Nights
of
Musk

Nights
of
Musk

Stories from Old Nubia

Haggag Hassan Oddoul

Translated by Anthony Calderbank

The American University in Cairo Press
Cairo   New York

English translation copyright © 2005 by
The American University in Cairo Press
113 Sharia Kasr El Aini, Cairo, Egypt
420 Fifth Avenue, New York, NY 10018
www.aucpress.com

Copyright © 2002 by Haggag Hassan Oddoul
First published in Arabic in 2002 as *Layali al-misk al-'atiqa*
Protected under the Berne Convention

First paperback edition 2008

Dar el Kutub No. 11464/08
ISBN 978 977 416 216 9

Dar el Kutub Cataloging-in-Publication Data

Oddoul, Haggag Hassan
          Nights of Musk: Stories from Old Nubia / Haggag Hassan Oddoul;
    translated by Anthony Calderbank.—Cairo: The American University in
    Cairo Press, 2008
                p.   cm.
                ISBN 977 416 216 1
                1. Arabic fiction-Nubia   2. Short stories, Arabic   I.
                Calderbank, Anthony (trans.)   II. Title
                892.73

1 2 3 4 5 6 7 8 9 10   14 13 12 11 10 09 08

Printed in Egypt

Contents

Translator's Note vii

Adila, Grandmother 1
Nights of Musk 29
Zeinab Uburty 41
The River People 89

Glossary 121

Translator's Note

The tragedy suffered by the Nubian people as a result of the construction of the High Dam at Aswan is one of the great untold stories of the twentieth century. And while details of Egypt's engineering triumph or UNESCO's efforts in relocating the ancient temples of Nubia, including the Great Temple of Abu Simbel, are there for those who wish to look them up, the accounts of the deep psychological and social trauma that this project left in its wake are more difficult to come by. It is difficult to imagine the enormous impact of the inundation of an entire ancestral homeland, consigned forever to the depths of Lake Nasser so that electricity can be generated and the mood swings of the mighty River Nile controlled.

Haggag Hassan Oddoul's four stories from Nubia tell of this tragedy, and though there are glimpses of the antediluvian days of Old Nubia in two of them, "Nights of Musk" and "Zeinab Uburty," the overwhelming impression is one of loss and bereavement. They are beautiful stories, clear, down to earth, fast moving, and easy to read. There are no literary pretensions. The writing is fueled by the raw power of human experience. The descriptions and images are highly sensuous, vividly conjuring up the sights and sounds of Nubia: the dancing, the music, the appearance and dress of the people and their environment are all brought to life in the reader's mind's eye. Even the Nubian language, ancient and precariously hovering on the verge of extinction, plays a role. Oddoul lets us use it and understand it. Its wonderful expressions and exclamations—immmmm! ibibibib!—begin to roll off our tongues.

The stories present wholesome challenges to the translator: grandmother speaks poor Arabic—she calls men 'she' and women 'he'—so she must speak poor English too. Nubian words are included in the Arabic text in a way that makes their meaning clear, so the English text must do this also. The use of onomatopoeia in the title story inspires the reader of the Arabic to pronounce the sounds out loud, and I hope that is what the reader of the English will do, for these are tales rooted in an oral tradition and they should be freed from the written page and spoken into the air.

The dilemma is that these delightful stories are born of a tragedy that can never be undone, and though there is humor, even a sense of hope in them, and though we may well enjoy them, we are left somehow confused and dismayed at the end. The Nubian people will be forever dislocated, their language is in danger of extinction, their culture and customs may fade away and the mellow molasses darkness of their skin may melt and mingle with the Egyptian shades of the north. But we can thank Oddoul and others like him that the Nubians will not go uncelebrated, for he has documented his people's demise and given us a taste of how things used to be deep in the south of Upper Egypt.

Adila, Grandmother

I sat on a stone by my grandmother's freshly-dug grave before the dry sands that stretched as far as the eye could see. She had been buried the previous night. Some distance behind me, the tiny houses of the exiles' village were clustered. I recited the Fatiha with tears in my eyes, and then I smiled. Who could think about the old woman and not smile? God have mercy on you. How I hated you, Grandmother, when I first visited the village.

When I arrived with my father and saw everyone hugging him, I felt like an outsider and was actually frightened by the dark faces. I wasn't that old at the time and the people of the village greeted me casually, with a slight upward movement of the chin. Deep inside I felt they disapproved of me. A woman as tall as my father, and with the same swarthy darkness, hurried over. She threw herself upon him, greeting him tearfully in Nubian. My father brought her over to me.

"Mohamed, say hello to your Auntie Awada."

My aunt lifted me up and hugged me so tightly that I felt her heartbeat in my breast. I liked her from that moment.

We went into the house followed by a crowd of men, women, and children. In the long narrow yard, everyone headed for the shade under the roof made of palm fronds. I could not see my father in the crush. Some inner urge made me turn my head from the grown-ups, and I looked toward the children. There I saw two eyes fixed upon me. When I caught sight of the girl a little younger than myself, she lowered her gaze shyly.

My father was kneeling on the palm mat embracing a skinny body in a black gallabiya. My aunt took my hand. Father made room for me, and I saw my grandmother for the first time. A dark, old woman with a shriveled face and sharp features. From under a scarf the color of her face, a woolen shock of red hennaed hair peered out like a flame. My aunt said, "Mother, this is your grandson, Mohamed."

The old woman looked at me through her narrow eyes. The sight of their whites flowing into the blackness of her pupils made me feel sick. She snarled and stuck out her lower lip in disgust.

"Immmmmm. You Mohamed? The gorbatiya's son?"

Everyone else laughed, but I was very upset. I knew this word 'gorbatiya.' It is a bad word that is used to put down anything that isn't Nubian. It is said with pride and superiority. I winced at my father's embarrassed laughter and looked hatefully at my grandmother. If I hadn't felt so out of place among that black crowd I'd have answered her back with even stronger words of my own. I almost cried. Then I felt my aunt's hand comforting me, and I looked up at her. There was encouragement in her eyes. Suddenly, my grandmother grabbed me, and I fell forward. She kissed me as if she were biting me. My nausea increased.

My aunt took me outside the house, where the children were talking about my father, who wore dark glasses and had come to visit his family after many long years away.

My aunt introduced me to the girl who had been following me with her eyes.

"Mohamed, do you know her?"

I shook my head.

"She's Zeinab, the daughter of your uncle Awad, God have mercy on his soul."

Zeinab looked silently at the sand, while I watched her face. My aunt held us against her tall body. We just about came up to her waist.

My father gave me a whole pound, but I still told him menacingly with tears in my eyes, "Mother said not to leave me with them."

"Your grandmother wants you to stay with her. I'll come back soon."

Because everyone, young and old, called my Aunt "Awada," I started calling her Awada too. She was so glad I was there. She took me around to all the houses in the village. With every Nubian we met, she stopped me and gave me a lesson on how he was related to us. This is one of my great uncles because his grandmother was my grandfather's aunt's daughter. And this is one of my great aunts because her mother was my grandfather's brother's aunt's daughter on the father's side. And that great aunt was originally from the same branch as our great grandfather, the founder of our tribe.

That is my so-and-so because such-and-such . . . and that is my such-and-such because so-and-so. . . . And of course all the children are cousins, because and because and because. She insisted that there wasn't a stranger among us. We were all one family and children of the same tribe.

After a week my hatred for the village had started to fade. I got used to their kabid bread and the green leafy soup they called ittir. I played with the children, who spoke both Nubian and Arabic. I quickly picked up Nubian words, especially swear words. We played football everywhere, since the village was surrounded by dry sand on all sides. After the game we would head for the nearest house and storm inside. All the houses had their doors open, or at least ajar. We would take great gulps of water from the cold jars. In the beginning I looked worriedly at the owners of the houses. I thought they might be angry at us charging into their homes, but I soon realized that no one minded. It was a completely normal occurrence. The village children belonged to everyone.

But there was no love lost between me and my grandmother. I detested her. I used to say, "If that wrinkled old woman dies, then I'll love this village." We were sitting for afternoon tea when Zeinab came in quietly. My grandmother sat her down beside her. She laid a pile of the breadsticks my father had brought in front of her. I was so jealous of quiet Zeinab. My grandmother loved her deeply. That night, on the bed made from palm stalks, Awada insisted I sleep next to her. She said to me, "Mohamed, your grandmother loves you as much as Zeinab, but she's afraid the same will happen to her as happened to me."

I stared at her searching for an explanation. She smiled and closed her eyes to sleep.

After the football match, we piled into old Halima's house. I saw her looking at me as if she'd forgotten that Awada had introduced us. My friend Ismail introduced us again. The old thing muttered contemptuously, "Immmmmmm." Then she turned her face away.

I told Awada, "Your relatives don't like me."

"Who told you that?"

"Most of the old ones despise me. They say 'immmmmmm.'"

"Don't worry."

"Is it because I'm white?"

"Some of us are white, Mohamed."

"Because my mother's a gorbatiya?"

"Mohamed, be quiet."

"My mother's better than all the women in this miserable village, and prettier than all of them too. If any child ever says my mother's a gorbatiya again, I'll hit him."

"Hit him then. You're a real Nubian just like us, Mohamed. Your father's Nubian. This village is your village. These are your roots."

Although the people of the village were inclined by nature to smile and show their gleaming teeth, they were always sad and desperately silent. They had a constant habit of sucking their lips when they felt sorrow. Even when totally alone a person might talk to himself and then suck his lips and let out a heavy sigh, inevitably followed by the words: "I ask forgiveness from God Almighty."

Two things struck me during my first visit. The first was how these people avoided becoming extinct. There were many deaths among them and funerals were always crossing the sand. Never a week would pass without their dark women in their black clothes rushing to the house of someone deceased, aligned in grieving rows, weeping, screaming wildly and wailing: Ibiyuuuuuu ibiyu! The second thing was that all these funerals took place, but my old grandmother wouldn't die!

Sitting down to tea with milk in the morning and the afternoon was an important ritual. The family would be gathered in harmony and affection. They savored tea like addicts. Any Nubian could go without his midday meal but no one would miss morning or afternoon tea. If circumstances left him with no choice, then he would suffer a terrible headache all day, and no glass of tea later on could help.

One afternoon they were all around the teapot. I came in late and sat down. My grandmother was screaming at Awada and crumbs of breadstick flew from her mouth in all directions. Awada was angry and she answered my grandmother, "Mohamed's fault ka kummo."

I understood. My aunt was saying, "It's not Mohamed's fault." I was surprised to see Zeinab looking reproachfully at my grandmother and repeating in her delicate voice Awada's words.

"That's right, Mohamed's fault ka kummo."

My grandmother rolled her lower lip in disgust. "Immmmmm. Nonsense, nonsense." Then she looked at me with those eyes of hers and that stomach-turning look and screamed, "Your mother gorbatiya. She took your father away from his people."

I left the tea and the breadsticks and went out. I heard Awada and Zeinab venting their fury at my grandmother.

I hated my grandmother more and more. Sometimes I'd watch her dozing on the palm mat. With her dark face she looked like Zeinab, except that her temples were marked with lines from a bleeding-blade. She slept on her right side, and always covered her face with her scarf to keep the flies off. By her side lay her amazing shoes. They were made of black plastic and were ancient. They had faded and turned the color of rusty iron. They were torn at the front and they looked like they had hideous gaping mouths. They were her feared weapon. Any famished goat that wandered into the open house in search of something to eat, if only a piece of newspaper, would be bombarded by her shoe and run for its life. It was the same with the dust-colored dog. He had been hit so many times that he now realized how dangerous she was. He would come into the yard and as soon as my grandmother lifted up a shoe, he would yelp with pain and turn in flight.

One day my grandmother went off barefoot to pay a call on someone in the village and left her shoes behind. With the tips of my toes I picked up one of them like a football and tossed it into the air. Each time, it landed on the floor upside down or on its side, but then quickly returned to its natural position. It infuriated me. I tossed it up a dozen times but the damned thing always landed the right way up with the gap in the front grinning at me. I hated even her stubborn shoes.

7

We came out of Zeinab's house. Her mother was always affectionate and playful with me. She asked me to eat with them and then insisted I sit next to Zeinab. I was aware the whole time of Awada staring at us. Her kind face gave a smile of approval. On our way back I said, "Awada, Zeinab's not black."

Awada smiled and tugged my ear playfully. "Mohamed, our village has girls of every color—black, tan, bronze, and white too. Pick the color you like, but don't ever do what your father did and marry a gorbatiya."

That night as I slept by Awada's side, I wondered. Awada had said my mother was a gorbatiya but I hadn't been angry with her. I had even laughed.

In the heat of the game, I collided with Younis, and he fell on the floor. He glared at me and said, "Penalty. It was your mistake, gorbatiya boy."

He stood up. I dislocated my finger when I punched him and knocked him back down onto the sand. Then my eyes puffed up from his brother Radi's punches. Ismail helped defend me. I ran home in tears. There they had heard about the fight from Zeinab. Awada rushed out threatening the brothers' family with misfortune. It was the first time I had seen her so worked up. My grandmother took hold of my hand and put my injured finger back in place. She looked at my eyes, then said, "Your eyes fine. Thank God!"

I told her how Younis had called me a gorbatiya boy so she cursed his father, "Younis . . . curse his father. Her brother Radi hit you too, curse her father too."

8

Her eyes no longer made me feel sick, and I relaxed in her arms.

I woke up at dawn to go to the toilet and found the front door open. I heard my grandmother mumbling. She was sitting on the prayer mat by the door. Silently I sat down on the step behind her. She completed her prayers and then raised her hands in supplication. "Wo Nor . . . O Lord . . . Wo Nor . . . O Lord. Bring no scandal upon us . . . Wo Nor. All will be well." Then she looked at the pale horizon and mumbled a Nubian ballad that I have since heard many times.

Ya salaaaaaam, the Nile and the palms,
   the long bank and the buoy,
Ya salaaaaaam, the mountains and the camel,
   a glimmer of hope, and the hamlet of Bahjura.

My friendship with Ismail and the brothers Younis and Radi strengthened. We played on the endless sands surrounding the village, jumping over the irrigation ditches, which were dry and cracked from the hot sun and the lack of rain. We picked wild devil fruit and crushed them with our bare feet, and they exploded into hundreds of pollen strands floating gently through the air to unknown destinations. The boys cursed me in jest as the gorbatiya's son, and I pretended to be angry. We wrestled and got sand in our mouths and swallowed our salty sweat.

We ran into my grandmother's house for water. Ismail threw the water left in the jar in my face and said, "Drink that, son of a gorbatiya!"

While we were laughing, Ismail let out a shrill scream. We caught sight of the iron shoe bounce off his back, hit the wall, and fall into the large water jar.

"Curse your mother, Ibn Diheyba."

My grandmother had heard Ismail calling me names, and she sent her shoe against his back. We ran outside the house laughing. I said, "I'll bet you anything my grandmother's shoe is the right way up in the bottom of the jar."

We crept quietly through the house and four heads peered over the rim. We burst into renewed laughter. The amazing shoe was there on the bottom, the right way up.

"We will send him back with the first person who is leaving." My mother ignored the telegram that answered her own message demanding my hasty return. She made my father come and get me. My grandmother spoke to him in Arabic so that I could hear every word.

"Lazyhead, listen. Mohamed in summer. Him come, him come to us. Or end up gorbati. Like mother."

When we got on the bus, my grandmother shouted: "Adila, Mohamed. Adila, Mohamed." On the train I asked my father, "Why didn't Awada marry?" My father was taken aback. He didn't answer my question. Instead he said, "My mother was praying for you when she said 'Adila.' It means 'Return, safe and sound.' But your mother doesn't want you to come and see my family in the exiles' village at all. The two of them are impossible. And it's all over you."

I got angry with him. I turned my face away and said to myself, "He's afraid of his own mother and he's afraid of mine." I turned up my lip in disapproval . . . immmmmm.

The next holiday Awada chided me. "All day you play with the boys and ignore Zeinab."

I answered her with the Nubian arrogance I had acquired. "I am a man. I don't like playing with girls."

Awada was annoyed, but then she laughed, "Nonsense, nonsense."

I hurried down to the corner of the street. The men sat in little groups, leaning against the walls of the houses. They were joined in the shade by a few skinny goats and some lean dogs. I sat a few meters from them with Ismail. The men were angry, discussing this new village of theirs and the desert land that so far had yielded only rocks and stones. They wondered about the water, and when it would arrive to wet the cement channels, which had cracked from the lack of moisture. My father took out a pack of cigarettes and offered them to the group. Ravenous fingers took them up, and they were smoked heartily.

The battle with my grandmother began the next morning before the sun was strong. She insisted I carry a can like Awada and go off with her and a crowd of women, girls, and little children to fetch cloudy canal water for the jars in our houses. I refused. My grandmother continued to insist until Awada intervened on my behalf and begged her. My grandmother came out of the house with her shoe under her arm, furiously cursing the origin and descent of every diabolical gorbati.

Despite my mother's opposition, never more than a week passed after finishing school before I was on the train eager to leave for the village. My father could relax. He didn't have to face up to my mother. He just let the village's hold over me make her agree. In the village Awada would hug me and Zeinab against her body, and we came up to her waist. Very gradually, the mountain of hatred I bore toward my grandmother began to dwindle away. I mixed more with the villagers and slowly gained a deeper understanding of the barren poverty of their lives in a strange land.

So far, some of the village land had been cultivated, but most was still dust. From afar, it looked like a mangy scalp with patches of hair amid its baldness.

The rusty bus took us around the cemetery and down the straight road to the exiles' village. I could see Awada waiting at the bus stop in the distance. She took me in her arms. My father laughed. "Awada, you love Mohamed more than you love his father."

Awada whispered in my ear, "If she wasn't so shy, she'd have come to wait with me."

I smiled. I was dying to see Zeinab. We neared the house. My grandmother was leaning against the door. She was barefoot and with her hand she shielded her two sick eyes from the sun. She watched us as we approached, and I smiled at her. She returned my smile by curling her lower lip in disgust.

"Immmmmm. The gorbatiya's son. You come back, you ass!"

Then she took me in her fragile arms, and her woolen hennaed hair dazzled my eyes.

I began to accept my grandmother as part of my divine

fate. The anger and curses she directed toward my mother did not diminish. In fact, they increased. I went round to the house of my late uncle, Awad. Joy shone in Zeinab's face and in that of her mother, who disappeared to make lemon juice and leave me with her daughter. Zeinab's body had matured, and she was more bashful than ever.

While we were drinking our morning tea, my grand-mother grew more and more furious. She was talking to Awada and my father in Nubian mixed with Arabic. I listened carefully and understood the gist of her sharp words. My great-aunt Halima had gone to the Egyptians' market to sell eggs and some chickens she had reared. It was a terrible disgrace. She was all alone and had no one to look after her. Everyone in the village relied on their children who worked in the north. Whoever had no support in the north reared chickens and sold eggs, and ate alone with no one to ask after them. It was a challenge for those people just to find the price of a spoon of sugar to put in their cup of tea.

My grandmother was furious. The clouds in her eyes grew thicker. She went on in Nubian, a spray flying from her lips. "Why have they driven us to this arid, God-forsaken place? Where is our old village? Where is our Nile? Where are our palm trees and our spacious houses? And the waterwheel? And the wedding parties full of food and drink and the beat of the tambourine? Where are the days of the flood and the days of the harvest? Where's our old village . . . the village of Bahjura?"

A stream of tears moistened the cracks on her withered face. Then she looked at my father, full of grief as she rebuked him.

"They've pulled us up by our roots, and we've become like brushwood. Our sons went off all over the place to work as servants in the land of plenty. They feed our grandchildren leftovers from foreigners and beys. And we here, they have thrown us into the valley of the demons. They gave us this land. Nothing grows on it but evil plants with bitter fruit that even the animals loathe. They've killed us, my son. The gorbatis have killed us."

My father looked at the ground. Awada's eyes were full of tears. Bewildered, I followed my grandmother's ugly eyes, from which sparks burst forth. She saw me looking at her, and she turned her gaze on my father. "Your aunts are hungry. They're selling eggs and chickens. It's a disgrace."

Then she looked at me and carried on in Arabic. "And you, lazyhead, you go marry gorbatiya. Immmmmm."

I no longer hated my grandmother. I accepted her curses on me and my father. But I couldn't contain my anger when she insulted my mother and showed me how much she hated her. She accused her of stealing my father from them.

My stock of Nubian words was piling up. The people of the village still made endless processions to the cemetery, with the women behind them wailing Ibiyuuuuuu ibiyu. My grandmother was determined to stay around. Her sight, however, was deteriorating. The shoes that had come like guided missiles began to go astray, and she had to locate her target through her sharp sense of hearing. She was opposed to the idea of traveling to the north for treatment with the gorbatis. She recounted the story of her late aunt, who had suffered the same symptoms in her eyes. The light of her

14

vision had faded until it went out completely. My grand-mother couldn't imagine that the people in the north, whom she hated so much, had a cure for her ailment. Awada begged her to go and have treatment, but my grand-mother resisted and reiterated that she was strong and well, had a good appetite, and still had all her own teeth. Awada importuned until my grandmother conceded, but only on condition that Awada did not travel with her. She wanted her to stay and keep the house open. She didn't like the idea of closing it up.

Awada was filled with anxiety. My father reassured her, saying, "Don't worry, Awada. I'll book her a place on the air-conditioned train. I'll take her to the best doctors. No expense will be spared. God willing, she'll come back fit and well. No . . . no . . . Awada. Mohamed's mother will be a daughter to her. She'll look after her just like you would. She may be a gorbatiya, but she's a kind woman."

The rusty old bus took us around the edge of the ceme-tery. In the distance I could still make out Awada and Zeinab waving to my grandmother. I couldn't imagine my grandmother in our house in Alexandria. I wondered if she would still insult my mother. By God, if the wizened old thing insulted my mother in our house I'd let her have it.

On the train, my father sat on the right hand row. My grandmother and I were on the left. My grandmother asked me, "Do you have tea with milk where you live?" My father went to the toilet. My grandmother was looking out of the window as if she could see. She turned to me suddenly and for the first time asked me about my sister. I forgot my father's warning. I was sleepy and I said, "She's getting married in two months to a gorbati."

My grandmother screamed ibiyuuuuuu ibiyu, terrifying me and the rest of the passengers. She stood upright, uncovered her red woolen hair and waved her black scarf in the air with an endless wailing of ibiyuuuuuu ibiyu, ibiyu-uuuu ibiyu. She stepped over me out into the empty aisle and began to dance the dance of the bereaved, beating its monotonous rhythm on the floor of the carriage. As the train sped along, her thin body, black veil, and sorrowful howls swayed in the air. She bumped into the row of seats. Some of the passengers laughed and some felt sorry for her. Girls, gripped by the fear that she was mad, cowered in their seats. Boys laughed at her. I watched her in amazement as I kept an eye on the carriage door through which my father would return. My grandmother reached the end of the carriage, turned round, and made her way back increasing the beats of her feet and her screaming. When she reached my seat and could see me she lashed out with her black scarf.

"Evil day, day you father marry you mother."

She turned around and continued her slaughtered dance. My father came up. He stood for a moment appalled, then he rushed to my grandmother. He took her forcibly and sat her down in her seat. He sat next to her, and I sat in his place. My grandmother cursed him in Nubian.

"Lazyhead, lazyhead, you married a gorbatiya and left us. Your daughter will marry a gorbati and be lost for ever. Yaseen went to a gorbatiya and left Awada to wither. So much for the gorbatiyas. They've taken my home, and they've taken those who would carry on our line."

My grandmother burst into a flood of tortured tears, and I cried with her, heedless of my father's threatening glances for having given my sister's secret away.

The atmosphere in our house was strained. My mother, who was ill herself, dealt with my grandmother cautiously, while my grandmother simply ignored her with scorn. My sister looked just like my mother and, unlike myself, had taken none of my father's color. She treated my grand- mother rudely and looked down on her. She was sorry that this old, black woman was her grandmother. She didn't even bother to greet her.

The operation was only a few days away. I was helping my mother understand my grandmother's way of speaking, especially the way she mixed up some of the letters and used masculine and feminine the wrong way around. My mother was trying particularly hard to make my grand- mother feel at home, not only for the sake of my father and me, but also because she was our guest. I was my grand- mother's guardian. I attacked my sister and threatened her if she tried to mock her. I looked reproachfully at my mother if she neglected or pretended to forget about her. They were both surprised at my behavior. I had told them angrily how she used to insult us and every gorbati in exis- tence. What was it that had changed me, and why was I now on her side?

One evening my mother moved up to my grandmother and said to her:

"The water on your eyes is white not blue. Don't worry."

"Not white, not blue, red . . . red . . . water color red. Blood in my eye, blood in every Nubian woman's eye."

That night my mother's illness grew worse. My father told my sister not to cry. "It's her usual illness. I'll take her to the doctor tomorrow morning." My mother took her medicine, but she continued to moan as we sat around her on the bed. My grandmother came in and felt her way along the wall. She sat down with us, and my sister muttered something to herself. After a few minutes, my grandmother placed her hand on my mother's head. She gave orders to my father in Nubian, and he quickly brought what she had asked for. A razor blade, alcohol, sheets of newspaper, a plastic ruler, and a clean cloth. My mother and sister looked at one another apprehensively, then their eyes bulged with terror as my father helped my grandmother turn my mother onto her stomach. They uncovered her legs and my grandmother moved forward with the blade. My sister tried to hold her back, but my father stopped her saying, "Leave her alone. She knows what she's doing."

My grandmother felt my mother's legs and with the razor blade she made quick cuts on her calves. Then she moved up to her back. She took the ruler holding it at both ends, bent it into a semicircle, and began to pass it along my mother's back and legs to gather the blood, which I then dried with the cloth. The blood continued to seep out from the wounds, and I kept drying it. My grandmother covered her legs and back with the newspaper, which soon turned dark red. She then moved the blade towards my fragile mother's temple. My sister screamed and my heart pounded. My father stopped her and said, "Enough." After a while they turned my mother over, and she yielded like a loose pillow. My grandmother poured the alcohol over my mother's head, neck, and chest and with her rough woody hands began to pull her flesh and knead it, while reciting verses from the Holy Quran. My mother could hardly open her reddened eyes. She looked menacingly at my father as if to blame him for his mother's barbarity. My sister could stand it no longer and she said to my father, "Get that crazy old woman away from my mother."

My father silenced her sternly. My grandmother didn't look at my sister, but as she continued to knead my mother's flesh and massage her scalp, she heaped curses upon her.

"Shut up gorbatiya donkey . . . curse you mother."

The next morning my mother awoke with her strength and vitality regained. I went into her room, leading my grandmother by the arm. We sat down next to her. My grandmother said, "Good morning, gorbatiya garri."

My mother looked at me and I said, "Garri means something like . . . stupid . . . foolish . . . ridiculous."

My mother looked at my grandmother for a moment then she laughed and hugged her and kissed her. That hug was the beginning of an age of harmony between the two antagonists.

The operation was a success. My grandmother recovered and began to see. She insisted on leaving, and my father got ready to take her despite my mother's demands that she stay longer. My grandmother told me why she was so keen to get away. She wouldn't be able to bear attending the wedding of my sister to a gorbati. And anyway she missed Awada. At the station, my mother and I stood next to her. My father looked at us. He couldn't believe the love that united us. My grandmother grabbed me by the hair and shook my head back and forth with her usual roughness. She said, "Mohamed, I love you, donkey. Come every summer to village. Visit us, you dog. See . . . we nice people."

"I'll come on condition that I eat ittir and kabid every day."

"Agree."

"I can play to my heart's content day and night."

"Agree."

"I don't have to fill the cans from the cloudy canal."

"Agree."

"You won't insult my gorbatiya mother."

My grandmother looked at my mother and winked at her then she pretended to put her foot down. "No . . . don't agree."

The following summer my grandmother was angry with me and my father because we hadn't brought my mother with us. She asked affectionately after her health and said to Awada that the gorbatiya was a wonderful daughter and the epitome of good morals and religious belief. Her only fault was that she was a gorbatiya . . . immmmmm.

That night Awada was more delirious than usual. She mentioned Yaseen's name several times. In the morning, she woke up late and found me sitting watching her intently. She said, "Why are you looking at me like that?"

"Who's Yaseen?"

She covered her face with her hand to hide her tears. I repeated the question.

"That's the third time you've asked me, Mohamed."

"You're always dreaming about him and calling his name."

"We got engaged, and then when they built the dam and our lands were drowned, he went north to make his fortune and then was supposed to come back and marry me. He never sent any money, and he never came back."

"If I were older and I wasn't your brother's son, I'd marry you myself."

Awada smiled and hugged me.

"You will marry me, Mohamed. You will marry me, my son, God willing."

I became friends with my grandmother. A seed of love grew in my heart. I looked forward to her jibes. I wouldn't feel happy unless she insulted me over afternoon tea when Awada and Zeinab were with us. I said to her one time, "If a Nubian marries a gorbatiya, why do they call their child 'half mule'?"

"Because it come half mule."

"So I'm a half mule?"

"Correct."

"Correct! So which one of my parents is the mule?"

"Your mother, you ass."

"Oh really . . . and why couldn't it be my fa . . . ?"

Before I could finish the word, I was on my feet making a run for it. I had almost slipped through the open door when the iron shoe caught me and rebounded against the wall. I peered cautiously inside. Grandmother, Awada, and Zeinab were in stitches.

I took to wearing the Sudanese gallabiya and the multi-layered turban, which they called kaseer. I began to love everything that was southern. I spoke broken Nubian, due to its difficult grammar, though I could understand much of its vocabulary. You could find me with the men, complaining like them of our new land that spewed stones and choked the palm shoots. I put up with my grandmother's complaints about the cramped house she lived in, which was jammed right up to the neighbors' houses. In Nubian she said, "Mohamed, I ask our Lord that I may die in our old country, in the village of Bahjura. I want to be buried in our cemetery on the hill that overlooks our Nile and our palms and our houses and our fields . . . amen."

I had two more years to go before I finished university. But Zeinab had blossomed.

One day my grandmother said bluntly, "Immmmmm, gorbati, peace of mind damo. No peace of mind."

"Why grandmother?"

"Awada say, Zeinab wait for Mohamed. I afraid Mohamed leave him, marry gorbatiya like her father and her sister."

The day I left for Alexandria alone my grandmother was even more distressed as she bade me farewell with her usual invocation. "Adila, Mohamed. . . . Adila, Mohamed."

I spoke to my mother about marrying Zeinab. She was silent. My sister was furious and rejected the idea outright in her usual off-hand manner. My father happily agreed, said it was the best thing I'd ever thought of, and then asked God to have mercy on his brother Awad's soul. The following summer my father read the Fatiha. Zeinab was mine. My grandmother hugged me for a whole hour. She wouldn't let me leave her side the rest of the day. She made me and Zeinab sit next to her on the palm mat. She prayed for us, and at sunset when Ismail came to take me out, she couldn't resist an insult before she let me go. "Off you go, lad. Yes, you gorbati, but by God, you good boy. Go with you friend and our Lord preserve you, half mule."

No one was happier than Awada, for Zeinab was almost an extension of herself. She was the new generation ready to bring forth a flood of life after Awada had grown old and barren and endured an arid age. So I was Awada's fiancé and her son at the same time. Awada became years younger, filled with joy. One night, she called me Yaseen, and we laughed. She wept and then laughed again. She wound the kaseer around my head and happiness almost leapt from her eyes as she told me how handsome I was, just right for Zeinab.

Old age laid hold of my grandmother. Always sitting in the shade, she gave praise to her creator, wo nor wo nor. I agreed with my father when he said that she didn't have long to go.

I went back to visit them with my mother. She was very worried, as if she were about to land on another planet among aliens. They received her with warm affection. My grandmother gave her a long embrace. Awada had dyed her hair with henna like my grandmother and it blazed like a bright red fire. She quickly befriended my mother and stayed next to her the whole day. My mother was comforted, and she liked the village despite its poverty and barrenness. She gladly accepted my grandmother's sharp tongue.

The days passed. As we sat one afternoon drinking tea, I tried to get my grandmother to say something. "Today my mother cooked something that no Nubian woman has ever dreamed of."

My mother was embarrassed. Awada smiled silently. My grandmother took the comment to be an insult to Awada and all Nubian women. She tapped her spoon against the tray, and it seemed to me like the bell for round one of a boxing match. She pointed to my mother as if she were accused of committing ten mortal sins. Then she looked at me.

"Your mother."

"What about her?"

"Know how cook okra. Know how cook ittir?"

"No."

"Your mother. . . . Know how bake kabid?"

"No."

"Your mother."

"Enough grandmother."

"Know how sow? Know how reap?"

"No."

"So why your father lazyhead marry him?"

My mother joined in our laughter and my grandmother relaxed in her victory. Then, in order to put my mother at her ease, she went on, "Mohamed stupid boy. She get curse for her father and her mother."

The telegram came one winter evening. We closed the flat and the three of us left the next morning. The following afternoon, we were in my grandmother's room. Two days before, the doctor had said she was dying. Her eyes were open, but she didn't see us. She saw those who had already passed away and were now coming to meet her: her parents and grandparents, her son Awad, Halima who had died of a broken heart. She talked to them and told them in a whisper that she was on her way and would see them in the shade of her grandfather's doum tree. My father was by her side reading the Holy Qur'an. My mother grieved as deeply as Awada and Zeinab. At sunset my grandmother revived a little. She recognized us and answered our greetings in a feeble voice. She sat up and got out of bed. She wanted to go outside. My father wept and said it was her final spurt of life. They wrapped her in a blanket. She lent on Awada and the two of them went out, with us behind. The desert cold gnawed our bones. My grandmother pushed Awada away and headed toward the sun, whose bleeding disk reddened the dry sand until it was the color of her flaming hair, for her black scarf had slipped off.

She moved as if she was learning to walk. She was savoring every breath. She called out, speaking in Nubian. "Wo nor . . . wo nor. Awada, can you see our palm trees standing row upon row? The date season, Awada, and the village of Bahjura in the feast. There is so much goodness, my girl. Yaseen will come back with his fortune and marry you. Wo nor . . . wo nor. Our Nile is sweet and kind. The buoy is still dancing. The village ancestors are sitting under my grandfather's doum tree. Is that a boat's sail? Is it coming for me? Awada, it's come to take me, Awada." She stumbled. Awada tried to support her, but she pushed her away and moved on a few steps, her arms outstretched, hurrying towards whatever it was she saw coming. Wo nor . . . wo nor. Awada couldn't reach her, and she fell on her face like a hollow palm trunk. They turned her over. There was sand on her face and in her open mouth. The dry yellow grains dotted her pupils and soaked up their moisture. She had given up the ghost, but not with any bitterness. Her face was a pharaonic statue, mindful of an existence far beyond our own, gazing at the horizon and those whom she could see waiting there.

She was quickly made ready. They put her on the bier. I was among her pallbearers. The night lay cold and heavy on the dry yellow sand and blackened it with a fearsome darkness. The wailing ibiyuuuuuuu ibiyu shrouded everything.

The sun came up and beat down on my head. I sighed as I stood up next to the grave to return to the exiles' village. The three days of mourning passed. My studies and my father's work forced us to leave. Awada was in tears as she bade her warm farewell to my mother and father. Then she clasped me to her right side and Zeinab to her left. We were as tall as she was. With our faces on either side of hers, her tears ran down our cheeks. In spite of her weeping, she emitted an aura of serene contentment and a loving smile fluttered about her lips.

The bus sputtered into action. My mother embraced Awada and Zeinab once more. She said to Zeinab, "My daughter, you and Mohamed will be married soon, God willing. Your wedding night will be here in our village, in grandmother's house."

The bus pulled away. From the window I saw Awada's scarf fall away to reveal a mass of red woolen hair, wrinkles, and the marks of the bleeding-blade on her temples. I could not tell if it was my aunt . . . or my grandmother.

The bus shuddered as it moved along. We waved to them and they waved back. They faded into the distance, and we went down past the cemetery. The tomb stones came into view, and we caught sight of my grandmother's grave. My mother wept and my father struggled to hold back his tears. My grandmother's face was merging with the face of my aunt before me. I smiled as the taste of tears filled my mouth, and I muttered, "Adila, grandmother."

Nights of Musk

L ong, long ago, south of the rapids, the nights exuded incense and oozed musk. They were watered by the celestial majesty of the Nile and nourished by the green strip of life that lined its banks. Their sky was pure and their air invigorating. There was born generation after generation, dark, dark. We would say: "We are dark, dark, for our sun shines upon our faces."

Aaaaaah Aaaaaah Aaaaaah

My wife was screaming in pain inside the house. Outside, in the wide courtyard, I sat under the arbor with my family around me. Anxiety gnawed like a frozen blade in my heart. The experienced men offered the usual words of encouragement. "Don't worry, they are the pains of a first birth. You'll soon be a father, Ibn Zibeyda." My uncle Bilal said, "Take this cigarette. Smoke it and learn patience." He leant over and whispered in my ear, "It's packed with the best bango. It'll calm your nerves."

Salha's screams and groans came from the distant room and seared me. She walked up and down the room wailing, supported by the shoulders of her mother and my sister, waiting for the fetus to fall and the swollen belly to relax. Water was boiling on the fire. Salha would not lie down until the time came. I was waiting to hear a sound sweeter than the roll of a drum:

Waaaaah waaaaah waaaaah

Duum-taka dum-tak duum-taka dum-tak

In the groom's house that night, the young men were warming up the drums, trying them out, *duum-taka dum-tak*. Even before we reached puberty I was trying to woo Salha, sometimes politely and other times rudely. I pursued her constantly. I strutted proudly before her at every wedding and danced for her. I sang her the ballad "Your breasts are firm like oranges." She had a magnificent chest. Her bouncing breasts drove me wild. They kept me awake at night and haunted me during the day.

The sunset twilight drew a line of watery red along the horizon. A young girl ran across the low sands up toward the village. I jumped out from behind a wall. She fell onto me and I was delighted. She was horrified and screamed: "Bismillah!" Sweat ran down her face and neck like branches of the Nile. She pushed me away and cursed me. "Devil, you're always on fire, Ibn Zibeyda."

I answered as I did every time. "Don't blame me. Blame the sun that won't let us cool down. Blame your bouncing breasts."

She hid a smile and ran off, and the hot thud of the tambourine resounded with the beat of my heart:

Duum-taka dum-tak duum-taka dum-tak

Aaaaaah Aaaaaah Aaaaaah

She screamed in the room, leaning on shoulders, moving exhausted up and down. Outside in the yard, I was waiting for the expected one to appear. My sister's son Habboub was learning to walk. He fell over and his vest came up and revealed his ebony body. He smiled at me. His tiny soft penis was covered with specks of sand. I went over to him. "You, my lad, are three years older than my daughter who's going to be born any minute now. I wonder . . . will she be for you? Will you chase her across the sand dunes and behind the palm trunks? I wonder if you'll woo her politely or provocatively? Habboub, she will have heavy breasts like her mother's. Will you sing for her 'Your breasts are firm like oranges'?" I lifted him up, and he was still smiling at me, trying to take the cigarette out of my mouth. "Little bastard. Make sure you don't go pestering my daughter rudely." I slapped him playfully on the thigh. A fresh wave of screaming brought me to my senses.

Weeeek Weeeek Weeeek

Hooooi hoooi hooooi

Fawziya hooi, Binyamin hooi, Salha hooi, Ibn Zibeyda hooi. That's how we called to one another as children, boys and girls, running over the soft glowing sand. We drew pure air into our chests and counted the colors of the magic Nile. From the top of the mountain, it wound its way into the distant blueness of the sky. Parts of it were sheets of silver reflecting the sun's rays. As we ran down toward it, its color darkened to intermingling shades of gray. We ran to it through the green bank, and it turned muddy brown. Naked we dove in and found it clear and pure. Wonderful Nile, mighty as the sea. When we got tired, we would stretch out on the bank, and the sun would take us in a warm embrace. The burning fiery rays caused a reaction inside us, and we grew up fast. The girls ripened in a few years, still young, and the older boys snatched them up at fabulous weddings. No one can imagine how delicious the taste of those weddings was without actually experiencing them. Wonderful, sweet, and wild are the weddings of the south.

And on the palm-stalk bed, leg wraps around leg and embrace follows embrace. Bellies swell and the dark-skinned generations come forth, carrying the sun in their faces, screaming:

Waaaaah waaaaah waaaaaah

Eeeeshshshsh eeeeshshshsh eeeeshshshsh

The rustle of the ears of corn, the branches of the trees, the leaves of the blessed palm, and the ripple of the Nile's gentle waves are questions that do not wait for answers.

The floods passed quickly. The women ululated joyfully at the luscious bunches of dates. Real seasons. We grew up in an instant, Salha. So many presented themselves to your father, and of all the lads obsessed with that magnificent chest, you smiled bashfully only when my name was mentioned. Ibn Zibeyda. You were mine and I was yours. And the happy wedding day finally arrived.

We don't know where the days come from.

And we don't know where they go.

Eeeeshshshsh eeeeshshshsh eeeeshshshsh

Ya salaaaaam ya salaaaaam ya salaaaaam

On moonlit nights, my friends and I, young lads happy at the first hairs sprouting on our lips, would sit under the two doum trees, singing the ballad of "The Dark Beauty," which lavishly celebrated the face of the dark-skinned beloved without naming her. Nearby, under the towering sycamore, you were sitting with the girls, virgins full of desire, enraptured by the effusive beats of the tambourine. Each one of you thought the ballad was for her. There was passion in the hoarse voice of our singer, who began like all balladeers south of the rapids begin: Ya salaaaaam. Everyone becomes enraptured, and why not? For al-Salaam is one of the names of God. We joined in enthusiastically, singing Ya salaaaaam after every line, like real professionals. The opening ya took our bodies forward, leaning toward you. The s was from Salsabeel, wellspring of Paradise. The *l* poured full and fat from moistened mouths, the long *aaaaa* ascended with the rising of our hands to our temples, next to our eyes and dropping lashes. The wide sleeves of our gallabiyas hung calmly, relaxing with the sweet long vowel, as it took away the heat from our loins and soothed our passion. And with the final *m* the hands fell quickly down to show how much, how much we enjoyed the song. We captured your hearts, and they poured forth a flood of potent giving. Your bodies swayed from side to side, and you clapped your henna-dyed hands to the rhythm of the tambourine's beat. We communicated, and in spite of the sandy distance between the doum and the sycamore, we were one harmonious group, swimming altogether through the heaving sea of the night. We dissolved, sparkling with burning desire and an ardent longing to be lawfully joined on a day we prayed would come soon.

Our grandmothers sat close by. They saw our shapes clearly and smiled. They whispered of their own days that had passed like a sweet dream whose moon has evaporated behind a single sunny day. They looked at the new generation blooming, and with their gleaned wisdom, anticipated what would come to pass between us one day. "Fawziya is for Binyameen, Nebra Tari is for Husayn the omda's son, Hawa is for Selimto, Salha is for Ibn Zibeyda . . . ."

Ya salaaaaam ya salaaaaam ya salaaaaam

Waaaah waaaaah waaaaah

Good news at last. I threw down the joint and leapt to my feet shouting, "He is the Giver, He is the Granter of all things, praise be to Him." My uncle Bilal, Salha's father, laughed and said: "Didn't I tell you to be patient?" Then, in tears, he embraced me. My sister Miska came out of the room drenched in sweat. She threw her arms around me and kissed me. "Congratulations to us all; you have a daughter, Ibn Zibeyda."

Waaaah waaaaah waaaaah

Dark dark dark

Dark faces, pure eyes, white teeth, and consciences. Our colors are primary and well-defined. We know nothing of twisted words and half measures. The crowning turban is as white and clear as the dawn, the gallabiya a cup of milk to cover us, the shoes bright red, the young women's kohl as black as night, the tattoos deep and dark. The gold is amber, dangling in rings from ears and noses, hanging upon the forehead, treasure upon a young treasure. It shines from the neck and falls playfully onto the unfettered chests, yellow and lucky, plunging, leaping about between the firm round hills. From the top of the head hangs the shaw-shaw, two bands of gold thread covered in beads that follow the movement of the head, dancing and colliding in the air, and making a *shaw shaw* sound.

Shaw shaw shaw

Taraaak trak-trak taraaak

The people are clapping, Salha. They are our people, the people of the south. It is the hands dance. They dance to the beat of their own hands, bringing their palms together with power and zeal. The resounding *taraaak* splits the air in the sandy courtyard under the gentle light of the lamps and the silver moon. *Taraaak trak-trak taraaak*. Everyone is here: men, women, children, old folk, and even the sick. There isn't a Nubian on earth who would miss a wedding. Our grandparents' souls watch contentedly from the cemetery, and when the dance heats up, they come down and mingle with us, longing to be among us again. A wedding party draws the whole village. Even the River People, inhabitants of the cool depths, emerge dripping from the water alone and in groups. We can feel them down on the bank of the river sitting in the branches and among the palm fronds. Their young alight on ears of corn, which dance in ecstasy beneath them and scatter drops of dew, like pearls, *eeeeeeshshsh eeeeeeshshsh*. We call to them. "Welcome amon nutto, welcome People of the River." The dance flares up and draws us into intense rhythmic passion, drowning in the thunderous roar of the tambourines *duum-taka dum-tak* and the explosion of clapping palms *taraaak trak-trak taraaak*. We disturb the spirits, the people of the nether world, Lord preserve us from their evil. They slip from deep under the mountain and burst forth like satanic shells from the cracks and crevices of the high peaks. They circle under the stars and then arrange themselves at the edges of the light, dancing and singing mischievously. Their voices echo through the bounds of space and a massive sound engulfs us. And we, in fear and trepidation, sing a prayer: "O God, O Protector, between them and us let Your protection fall."

Just such a night was our night, Salha. Your old mother and my sister with the women sprinkling salt and Daughter of Sudan perfume in the air. They danced the perch dance amid a crowd of women adorned with gold of all shapes and sizes, gleaming and rustling, *shaw shaw shaw*, and the silver anklets on their feet with a clear ring, *klin-klin klin-klin*.

That night, there wasn't a limp body, nor a languid heart, not a single person who did not take part, nor a single tongue that did not congratulate, not a single weary soul. Everyone joined in the dance.

They had a wonderful procession for us, sweet Salha, the bride and groom, and the women's ululations were like brass bells and bird songs.

Lilililililililililiiiiiiy

Dirgid-dirgid dirgid-dirgid

Her sprightly female donkey was carrying her across the rocks. Her mother had sent her to the next village, and now she was coming back. I was lying in wait behind a fold in the mountain, and she rode past me. I followed and she heard the hooves of my male donkey. When she saw me, she gave her donkey a violent slap and off it leapt over the rocky land, four pairs of hooves beating the rhythm, *dirgid-dirgid dirgid-dirgid*. She turned west and my donkey followed in full chase. The sand dunes started and the she-donkey slowed down as she climbed. I dismounted with the hem of my gallabiya between my teeth. Two steps and I put my hands on the donkey's rump, leapt up with my legs open, and landed on the back of the beast, right up against Salha's back. She screamed.

"Ibn Zibeyda, you filthy rascal, leave me alone!"

She cursed me while she tried to undo my hands from around her waist. The donkey was taking us round in circles, and Salha was losing patience.

"Ibn Zibeyda, someone will see us, then there'll be real trouble."

"No one can see us except God."

"Then may God roast you."

"He'll forgive me when I marry you according to His law, and Prophet Taha's law."

"Haa haa haa."

"Your breasts are firm like oranges."

I almost had the oranges in my hands when she sunk in her ivory teeth and elbowed me sharply in the side. My hands let go, and with a push of her back, she sent me rolling down the dune with sand pouring inside my gallabiya.

Salha laughed.

"Haa haa haa. That's so you'll learn some manners, Ibn Zibeyda."

Haa haa haa haa haa haa

Kum-ban-kaash kum-ban-kaash

The children joined in the fun. They drummed on old cans and sang and danced in the courtyard. Dancing and singing are in our blood. We inherit them. Children of the tribe, you have added joy to our joy at the birth of Zibeyda. Two young children came into the yard. One held a bottle between his hands while the other tapped marvelous rhythms with two spoons.

Kin-klin-lin kin-klin-lin kin-klin-lin

Immmmmm immmmmmm immmmmmm

The bride was sulking, refusing even to talk to her hot, impassioned groom. She even wanted him to pay her a real Turkish guinea just to start a conversation.

On the bed you were like dark nocturnal velvet to the touch. They had rubbed you all day with dulka oil from Halfa, with extracts of fragrant oils and herbs. Its sweet smell penetrated your pores and radiated from your body, as if the dulka oil was in you, not on you. I touched your shoulder with nervous fingers. They slid to your breast and your perfect stomach. You laughed as if I was tickling you and your braided African locks, shining with oil, danced about your head. Ah *aaaaaah* what a girl! How gorgeous you were! Your mother had used her own experience to bring you up to be polite and well-mannered, and then to teach you how to have fun on the palm-stalk bed. You surprised me, Salha. You were a whirlpool raging in the flood season, a lavish wave of giving, a lusty jet-black mare. When you turned your legs over and I saw you from behind, my heart leapt. Our bodies are so sweet, they need no words. Our weather is so perfect, we need no covers. The house was wide and spacious, warm and still, and the silence utterly complete, exhausted after a wedding that made the universe tremble.

Salha, you were a naughty little devil when you were a child, then you changed into a charming and understanding young woman. Your father Bilal gave his consent, and I took you in lawful marriage. And now here you are with me, naughty again as a bride. You've returned to your naughtiness, and now it is allowed. I prefer you this way.

Aaaaah aaaaah aaaaah

Tudishshsh tudushshsh

In the darkness before dawn, we jumped into the celestial Nile to perform our ablutions in its pure and holy water. It flows from the springs of Salsabeel in Paradise. The rippling water has its effect. It passes over our bodies and we absorb its silt and fertile mud. My pores draw it into my bones, into my marrow, and it kisses the water of life and gives it its dark color. It embraces your sweet body slowly and deliberately and seeps inside until it rests in the womb, enfolding the tiny beginning, giving it color. There it grows and curls up. And outside, the belly looks like a soft, round sand dune. And on the day God wills, our love comes out to us, a blessed child with the sun in his face, crying.

Waaaaah waaaaah waaaaah

Kum-ban-kaash kin-klin-lin kum-ban-kaash

I stood beside the bed. Salha was lying there exhausted, smiling contentedly, holding our child Zibeyda. Her father Bilal stood next to her mother. They were both delighted. Habboub, on his mother's shoulder, was shouting happily and fidgeting. He wanted to get down and play with my daughter. I said, "Bismillah," and picked my daughter up in one arm and Habboub in the other. I whispered into his ear, "Habboub, if the Almighty grant that my daughter be yours, then take her in lawful marriage. Sing to her . . . 'Your breasts are firm like oranges.' She'll like that. And when she screams *weeeek weeek* and brings you the *waaaah waaaah*, a little girl with dark skin, and the sun in her face, call her after your mother, Miska al-Tayib."

Zeinab Uburty

Here we divide all living things into three. First, there are the adamir, the descendants of Adam, that is us. Half of us are evil like Cain, and half of us are good like Abel. Then there are the inhabitants of the river bottom, and they too are good and evil. The kind ones we call amon nutto, the River People, and the evil ones amon dugur, the River Trolls. We pronounce the word dugur quickly and violently to get it out of the way, as if it is a plague. But evil as amon dugur are, they only ever harm one or two adamir every so many years, either by taking them into their watery home by drowning, or by throwing the cloak of idiocy around them so that the person becomes an imbecile. Sometimes they snatch gold from women's wrists, but they rarely kidnap beautiful girls, and if they do they never keep them for more than a few days. However, the evil ones among the third kind of conscious beings, the People of the Current, are totally the opposite. I take refuge in God, the Almighty Protector, for they are godless infidels and are truly evil. Their malice towards the adamir is terrifying, and we are helpless in the face of their wicked powers. Because the balance of power between us and them is so uneven, God the Most Merciful has protected us, placing a barrier between us and them. It is true that they can see us while we cannot see them, but if you were to ask if one of them can ever cross the barrier, the answer would be, yes, in one case only: if a greedy human summons it using a book of magic and orders it to wreak mischief among his own folk. No sooner does the evil creature hear the summons than it accepts with a broad grin, its fiery body shaking with happiness. The naive human has broken the barrier, and he himself has summoned it in the hope of gaining good things from Satan! The end is always the same. The adamir are struck by a terrible plague, as are the two branches of the River People, and even the beasts and the insects and the crops as well. And the person who breaks the barrier drinks the bitter cup of despair, and lives the rest of their life alone, ostracized, in eddies of grief and streams of regret, before dying a horrible and shameful death. Then the devil records their name in the register of victims that every so often he takes up to his infernal master, Iblees, loathsome prince of the nether world.

The following events took place in our land, the land of Nubia, land of gold, near to the valley of Kallik at the foot of the mountain chain of Wawaat, where our village nestled peacefully, exactly in the middle of that vast distance between the first and second rapids on the mighty river of the world, the River Nile. They were related to us when we were young lads just about to mature by the late Hulla, who witnessed them as a small child. God granted him a long life, through one hundred and ten floods. From the age of ninety-nine he had nothing to do except sit and stretch out under the doum tree that was as old as himself and boast about the days of long ago and how the nights used to be. Then the world was really a world. The plants were greener and the dates were almost fingers of sugar. Meat tasted more delicious and people understood more. In those days, sexual intercourse really was sexual intercourse. And then he would slip into telling strange stories, like the story of Zeinab Uburty. The name filled us with terror. Hulla told the story with great passion for he had lived it, and it had stayed with him all the years of his life.

"We were people like any other people, a little better perhaps than most people. We prayed and knelt in prostration; we danced and debauched; we could be right or wrong; we got stoned and drunk; we planted crops and harvested; we got married and had children; in sum, we lived and died. Sometimes we would envy and hate one another, and when the boring monotony of our lives became too much, we'd think of some way to amuse ourselves. There would be a party to get merry and dance, or a woman would have a cursing match with her neighbor, or we would fight, man against man then house against house, but rarely did anyone receive serious injuries. The family elders would step in and make peace and enjoy their importance in the village. Then they would devour a slaughtered lamb, drink tea, and smoke huge cigars filled with bango. That's how we used to be. Until one year the pilgrimage season came around in

Kiyahk. Not a single man or woman set off for the Holy House of God, even though things were much cheaper in those days. And like every year, Touba followed Kiyahk. That's when strange events started to take place that made my hair turn white even though I was only a child. That Touba, boys, was colder than cold itself. We huddled inside our houses around braziers and ovens, for the sun had left us and had moved away to the farthest reach of the sky's dome and let through dark northern clouds that didn't normally appear. They veiled the blueness of the sky and only a little light reached us. Our entire day was gray. Imagine, you in this mixed-up generation today, every morning we would find the water in the pots and jugs and metal pans covered with an extremely cold glass-like layer. We had to break it to let the water flow out from underneath. We children used to suck the cold layer and crunch it, and it turned into water in our mouths, and we'd get stomach ache and bad bowels. By Almighty God it really happened, you bastards. The Nile itself, until well after dawn, was clothed in that translucent glass layer, which we have neither seen nor heard of before or since. With our very own eyes we saw dead fish, goggle-eyed in terror, motionless except for the motion of that layer. And after the strange substance went away we would collect the fish and eat them, grilled and fried over the fires by which we kept warm.

"We finished with the cold at the beginning of Baramhaat. It was as if that Baramhaat was a bench upon which to rest, for after it a scorching summer swept in with Barmouda. The sun came down so low that in the mornings, as it appeared above the horizon, its bloody halo collided with the summit of the eastern mountain. The mountain shuddered and bellowed before the horror that assailed it, and flaming rocks flew off and crashed down into the river, which passed directly below. We heard the sound of the water hissing from the fire: *tshshshsh tshshshsh tshshshsh*. At the same time, the earth rumbled in our village and the houses shook. The state of the speechless beasts would have touched an infidel's heart. The birds flew frantically west and bumped into one another, shrieking and calling for their little ones, who had fallen in shock from their nests to the ground. Our animals ran west too, and the lads followed them to stop them reaching the ravine. Then the sun leapt across the wide course of the river and passed over our heads, its halo transformed into a massive ball of dazzling silver fire, whose flames licked the air above us: *wshshshsh wshshshsh*. And then it continued its journey, passing quickly across the sky until it drew near to setting. The bottom of its halo, which had regained its bloody color, struck the top of Mount Wawaat and caused a second, stronger tremor. The birds took to the sky once again, and this time the animals fled east, and the lads had to stop them throwing themselves into the Nile and drowning. It was our good fortune, and yours too, that the peaks of Wawaat are several leagues away and that the blazing rocks that were falling landed far from the village. Otherwise we'd have all been incinerated like the people of Sodom and Gomorra, and we wouldn't have brought you into the world, and I wouldn't have to look at your stupid faces gaping at me. Anyway, the sun roasted every living thing. Our dark skins turned deep black. The dogs lay all day in the shade, panting, just like the goats and the sheep. The cows refused to work and turn the waterwheels. The camels lost their renowned patience. The donkeys . . . the donkeys, you sons of the tribe, refused absolutely to let us mount them. And if anyone who thought he was the local horseman jumped on their back, they'd bolt and throw him to the ground and try to kick him to death. The pigeons flew only for a few moments before sunrise and sunset. Any reckless young pigeon that flew out during the midday heat (and in fact, there was midday heat all day) would be broiled alive, feathers and all, and fall deliciously grilled to be eaten by the dogs and cats at night, because they couldn't bear eating during the day with the scorching heat. They were like us, like every living thing that moves on two legs or more, or even crawls on its belly."

Hulla straightened himself up, and slammed his stick down on the yard or so of sand that separated us from him. He looked into our startled eyes, and we watched him nervously.

"I swear I'd irrevocably divorce all my wives, and God have mercy on them, if the reason for our sun leaving its place that Touba, and fleeing to the farthest reach of the dome of the sky until it became smaller than a star, and then sliding so low in Barmouda that it sat on the tops of the mountains, if the reason for all that wasn't that despicable woman. And then there was the low level of the Nile and the putrid air and the dead crops that brought rats and lice and blood. The reason was that accursed woman. She was also the cause of all the hatred and malice among ourselves. Her name was Zeinab, Zeinab Uburty, preserve us O Lord. Hold on to your lucky charms and take refuge in God from the evil of His creatures, may she be damned in this world and the hereafter. . . . Anyway, the foolish woman sought the help of the perfidious devil Kakoky. It was in the autumn of that year that she uncovered a most unholy book, a book of magic. I'm going to tell you her story and our story, and if anyone laughs or interrupts, I'll clobber him over the head with this stick here. I will relate, and whoever believes, believes, and whoever doesn't is a bastard. Here is what happened.

"After the evening prayer, the chief watchman, who was of strapping build, went in to the youngest and newest of his wives. She mocked him and spoke to him rudely. The following night he went in to his middle wife and came back out with her snarling *immmmm* in agitated contempt. And on the night that followed that night, just as that night had followed the night before, he was forced to go in to his oldest wife, whom he had lately been avoiding, having deemed her too old. She laughed out loud at him and wiped the rugs on the floor of the room with his honor. Her words stung like a Sudanese horsewhip. The poor man had gone impotent. His palm tree, which had once stood so proud and erect, never flagging nor tiring, and had inspired such terror in his three wives and made them cry *eeeegh eeeegh* in great pain and enormous pleasure, was now all soft and limp, like the leather strap a teacher uses to hit the little children. It was a chance for his old insulted wife to insult him back.

"'Eeeeeeeh, you call yourself a man? You married two other women, a widow and a virgin, on the pretext that I didn't satisfy your virility. Well now you don't satisfy my womanhood. You, the man they call "Temple Door" because you're so big. It's my right to marry two men over you, a widower and a virgin.'

"He slapped her and she laughed a self-satisfied laugh. Then he wept.

"That's what happened to the chief watchman. The next one to be afflicted was Karmy the carpenter, the watchman's sister Bahiya's husband, then Abdullah the farmer, then so-and-so, then such a body. Every night a married man would go impotent and keep the terrible secret in his breast. Finally, they all confessed on the morning that Abd al-Aal, the barber and surgeon of the village, wept after his wife beat him and announced that he had become colder than his own blade.

"But what had happened, and what was the reason? No one knew. No one understood. From there, Uburty's happiest days began. But the old witch didn't know what disasters would happen to her at the end of her happy mirage. Anyway . . .

"In the bitter cold that had struck and confused us, the women were distracted and put up with the blight, but when the cold eased off in Baramhaat and before the boiling hot weather of Barmouda set in, they were screaming in distress, cursing the men. Some of the more vivacious ones started mixing with the older boys, who were like adolescent billy goats.

"And because our village knew nothing of magic and binding of males, save what we heard of happenings in nearby Egypt, and the villages in the Delta far away, not to mention the afflictions of black magic, news of which had reached us from the jungles to the south of the fourth cataract, everyone was terrified. The men's knees were weak and the women's nerves on constant edge. For without that sweet cursed thing that joins man and woman together, colors grow pale, and life's fire goes out. Lost are the evenings when the men brag of their prowess. Gone is the opportunity for a woman to boast how many times her husband can manage it, when all she wanted was to hide her disappointment with a useless man who can't satisfy her appetite. On top of all that was the abrupt halt in the production of the new generation, and the gift of procreation that our Lord has bestowed upon most creatures. You know how proud we are of our family lines, which we have decided are the most valuable of all family lines, and which the foreigners call the 'brown man's line.' Anyway . . .

"We told ourselves that we would have to be patient. The women too would have to be patient. The flood season was approaching, and as you may or may not know, the flood season is nothing more than the long, broad river's manhood overflowing his banks with the water of life. It mounts the land, and plants are born and udders grow fat. It's the season when bulls and billy goats get lusty, as do all male beasts, whether gifted with speech or not, and the wild animals in the mountains, and the birds, and the insects that crawl over the sand, even the creatures of the river. So what were the men worried about, and why were the women so upset? But . . . let's get back to Uburty.

"Her mother called her Zeinab. She grew into a thin, ugly girl. She was envious and spiteful. Her tongue cursed everything that moved, young or old, man or woman, respectable or otherwise, cow or goat. From early puberty she began directing curses at the men. She also included those women who stuck up for their husbands. Because she was so ugly, in looks and in nature—I ask forgiveness from God Almighty—no man stirred the pool of her womanhood. That was the main reason for all the perversions she thought up, and the problems she caused, and the battles she started, and the violent, bitter hatred she felt toward everything. So they called her Uburty. 'Uburty' is the word for the ashes that gather at the bottom of the household oven. Whenever there was a disaster or a catastrophe, the women would dig their hands into the uburty and pour it over their heads, and smear it on their faces till they looked hideous and disgusting. Then they would wail and scream, and dance the dance of the bereaved. That's why whenever the word 'uburty' was spoken, it was not taken to mean the remains of firewood, but rather everything that was evil and wicked and awful. That young woman had such bitter, twisted innards that her face was hideous and disgusting on its own. She well deserved the name Uburty. And what made it all the worse was that she was one of us, and we were her folk.

"She remained a spinster until she turned forty and married an old widower. She made his life a real misery. One day she went down to see him in his field. For no particular reason she cursed him and his mother Hajija (that is to say Khadija, as you pronounce it nowadays with your queer way of speaking), and because he so loved and adored his late mother Hajija, he couldn't control himself. He hit her in the face with the handle of his hoe and knocked all her teeth out except one, which remained leaning from left to right across her nauseating mouth. She spat out her broken teeth and spewed up some blood and then tore the hoe from his hands and hit him with the iron end right on the top of his head making a gash about half an inch deep. From that day on he suffered from a stammer and incontinence, salivated constantly, and had a twitch in his left side. He divorced her, and died two floods later—there is no power and no strength except through God. And from the curse of her slain husband, whose death went unavenged, her face grew uglier and uglier and became pock-marked, even though she had never had the pox.

"No other men presented themselves until she was almost fifty. She then gladly accepted Infirmary Mahmoud, a weak, sickly man whose dark skin had gone pale yellow. He was ten years her junior. He had presented himself in the hope that he would find someone to look after him, since his only sister had just joined his mother in the cemetery. He spent the summer in the village and the winter in Aswan Infirmary being treated for his chronic disease. Uburty never beat him, even though he was her lawful husband. That was because he was so obviously weak. In fact, such was her kindness that she sufficed herself with cursing his grandfathers and ridiculing him in front of other people. She would say, 'Ah, God rest my first husband's soul. That's what I call a man. He made me feel like a real woman.' She was exaggerating, of course. On his deathbed, her first husband had stammered out a confession that the main reason for the problems between him and Uburty was that she repulsed him. He couldn't go near her, despite her pleas. Then Uburty would carry on. 'I'd rather be divorced than have Infirmary's limp, bony body, and have people mistakenly thinking I've got a man.'

"Every night for years she sat, eaten up with hatred. She concentrated her envy on the women who were well tended by their husbands, and the same envy would gnaw at her insides. And as she thought how she might avenge herself against all women, she remembered that her mother had often talked about an ancient book of magic her grandmother had hidden. It was the last surviving book of magic from the collection of their great-grandfather, the evil wizard, Hamreen. It was he who had humiliated the men and tasted some of the women after bewitching them. But he left the rest, not because he was exhausted, or because his conscience disturbed him, but because he didn't find them pleasing. Then the villagers killed him and tore his body limb from limb. They buried it far away, deep in the mountains. The hyenas dug it up and ate it. Then a huge beast, the like of which had never been seen before, came and took Hamreen's skull in its mouth. As it closed its great jaws, the skull exploded with a terrifying bang. The beast raised up its muzzle, and the brain slid out of the shattered skull down into its throat. Then it began to break the bones, and they cracked in its mouth like the gunpowder of the French soldiers who had invaded Elephantine Island years before.

"Uburty took the book out of a hole by a tree above the vale of Kallik. She pored over it for three months during her husband's autumn sojourn in Aswan Infirmary. But, thanks be to God, she was unable to understand the book. She could hardly read, and the script itself was poorly written and difficult to follow. The pages were pale and crumpled, and her sight had always been weak. Besides, the spells and riddles it contained were far too complicated and profound for her simple, uninspired brain, which was as dull as her body. In the end she succeeded in mastering one chapter. She concentrated all her effort on it in order to quench her blazing desire for revenge. It was the chapter on binding the males.

"She laughed like a mad woman when she finally mastered it. At last, the chance was hers. And she swore an oath as she rubbed her tired eyes. 'I swear on my grandfather Hamreen's soul, no woman shall taste what I am deprived of. I shall begin with my cousin's son. The boy's father broke the tradition of the clan by leaving me, his cousin, and not taking me in marriage. Instead he went and married Fat Sikeena. He was a coward.' She spat on the floor. 'Ah . . . he died early, perhaps because I was always praying for evil to befall him. And now his son, the son of a bull and a cow, goes and marries once, then takes the beautiful widow, and makes them three with the young virgin. Ah . . . I'll start with him, the chief watchman, who's built like a temple door. And after him, his sister Bahiya's husband."

"By the beginning of Touba, she had bound all the husbands in the village. She had broken their spirit, and they went about with their heads hung low like dejected donkeys. The women were tormented by deprivation just like her. But because Touba was so cold, and everyone was so loath to remove any clothing whatsoever, the women were compelled to be patient.

"The cold became bitter and we were constantly shivering, every one of us, especially early in the morning, and in the evenings and all through the night our teeth would chatter. We were all making a rattling *takatakatakataka* sound. Our speech became interspersed with rattling and chattering, and it took weeks of practice for us to understand one another. If someone wanted to give the morning greeting, the words would come out like this: 'Takataka mas takataka kag takataka ru.'

"We even abandoned the use of gestures so that we wouldn't have to take our hands out from under our robes and shawls. In the end, we had to use eyebrow and lip movements and pucker our faces. The intelligent ones understood one another, but most people just became confused. They managed to get along, but deep inside, each cursed the other's stupidity.

"Each family slept in one room, in the middle of which was a brazier that never went out. There was another brazier in the bathroom. We weren't used to such pitiless cold in our hot land.

"The darkness was pitch black and silent. All that could be seen of Uburty as she stood in the yard of her house was a gleam of yellow in her eyes, and her leaning tooth. She read some spells, and muttered for a while. Sweat was pouring from her. She focused her eyes on some point up Mount Wawaat, and she could just make out the ball of fire that shot up from between the peaks of the mountain. In seconds it was above the yard. It descended to the ground and began to expand, turning into phosphorous gas that took the shape of a hideous body, taller than the tallest palm tree, mightier than the mightiest sycamore. After a moment the color became orange, and some parts were blue. His claws and horns were as black as carob pods. His bald head shone between the tips of his long, pointed ears, which quivered as he spoke. His eyes were narrow, vertical slits without lashes, his nose two digits wide, his mouth three. From the knees down, his legs were set into the sandy floor of the yard, yet he still moved with ease, as if he were standing in shallow water. It was the devil Kakoky, the one entrusted by Iblees, Prince of the Demons, with bedeviling and leading astray the people of Nubia.

"Kakoky began with a bellowing laugh. 'Ho ho ho ho ho.'

"That's how the godless devil laughed. Even though it was the second time Uburty had summoned Kakoky, she still shook with terror at the demon's massive size and booming voice, and the blasts of air that issued from his cavernous windpipe. She was also afraid that the villagers would hear what was going on, and her secret would be revealed.

"'Lower your voice will you, or they'll hear you.'

"'Have I not told you that no human can hear me except you, and that no one can see me except you.'

"'How could they possibly not hear all that terrible din? Listen, build me a house away from the village.'

"'Ho ho ho. Your wish is my command.'

"'And I want more gold, so that the men will find me pretty and the women will be annoyed.'

"'Ho ho ho. Your wish is my command.'

"'And a fine mule with a soft saddle that won't hurt the bones in my backside.'

"'Ho ho ho. Your wish is my command.'

"We were astonished when we saw on a hill in the distance tall, broad workmen, bare-chested in the freezing cold, building a strange-looking house with incredible speed. And where exactly? On the top of a hill that was difficult to climb, and well away from the village. We couldn't believe our eyes. Still, no man made the effort to ride over to the hill and find out what was happening. They said that the cold was more biting and intense in high, open places, but the truth was that they were terrified of the giant builders. We never imagined that the house belonged to Uburty. She came down to see us the following day on the back of a mule that was as fat as a cow and just a touch shorter than a horse. We were astounded. The mule bent down so that Uburty could get off his broad back. The smell of sweet perfume filled the air around her. She approached, smiling proudly. She was wearing all kinds of glittering gold ornaments. Around her legs were a pair of shining silver anklets that clinked against each other, and upon her shoulders a stole of fox fur, the like of which we had never seen, for the fur was thick, and as white as milk. Incredibly, it kept the cold away from Uburty so much that she was sweating. She moved with the sprightly grace of youth, although she was nearly fifty, and she invited us to enjoy food and drink in her new house. Then she returned to the mule, who bent his legs for her to jump up onto the beautifully inlaid leather saddle. A quick prod from her foot and the mule trotted off, faster than any mule we had ever seen.

"The village might have been grieving, but Uburty was in an excellent mood. The curse on the married men was complete, and so was Uburty's shining new appearance. She'd put on some weight as a result of eating five wholesome meals a day, even if her ugliness had not disappeared and would never do so. Because of the life of luxury she was now living, she wasn't overly bothered when no one accepted her invitation. To be quite honest, everyone thought there was something disturbing about the house.

"No one went down to the fields until midday, when the glass layer covering the Nile started to melt, and the trees and plants began to regain their steadiness after they had been shivering all morning, and their branches had clashed in a mighty rustling of leaves. Their fruit was all withered, and they moaned as if they were in the throes of death. In Amsheer the strip of cultivated land turned into a frozen green carpet. When you walked on it, the grass snapped and crumbled like breadsticks. The egrets, wagtails, and herons, and the other little birds, as well as the hawks, eagles, and kites of the mountains had all migrated from the village. All that remained were a few crows cawing, and one particularly large raven that never fell silent, day or night. He alighted on the gates of all the houses and danced and screeched. No one had any idea that it was Kakoky.

"At noon people would light small fires around the palm trees and fruit trees, so that they wouldn't die like the rest of the crops, which had frozen solid. The afternoons passed quickly, and the chattering of teeth would increase, the donkeys would start to shiver, and the dogs would howl as they rubbed up against their masters, desperate for warmth. Then everyone would run back up to their hamlets as they heard the rustling of the branches and leaves, and the chirping of the grasshoppers and the croaking of the frogs, who died every day in their hundreds and turned dark blue. Inside the houses, the women had already lit the ovens and braziers, and fires burned in the hearths. The women were like cabbages, wrapped in layer upon layer of clothing all covered with a red shawl. One sunset, due to the incredible bitterness of the cold and a shortage of firewood, an old woman who lived alone went crazy and actually set fire to her house and sat inside in order to keep warm.

"Early every morning, on her fat mule, Uburty would ride down from her hilltop to the strip of frozen green. She was oblivious to the cold and the biting wind of Amsheer, for the thick white fur of her stole kept her warm. All three of them were blissfully happy: herself, her infernal mule that was so strong and vigorous, and the demon Kakoky who had assumed the form of a raven, for that was the most appropriate and comfortable form for him. He flew above the other two, alighting now and then on the mule's rump or on Uburty's head to let out a great screech. Then they would go up to the village and move through the narrow alleys, while the people cowered inside their homes around their fires with their teeth chattering. They heard the hoof beats of the mule and the screeching of the raven, and their fear and anger grew, as did their suspicions of Uburty.

"That's how the months of Touba and Amsheer passed. They were the happiest Uburty had ever experienced. The evil woman, who had betrayed the clan, did not know that her inevitable fate, as decreed and recorded in the Lord's preserved book, was waiting for her after two more months. And two months isn't a long time.

"During those days, O you who no longer respect the old folk, the poisonous insects that crawl along the earth were frozen under stones and in crevices between the rocks. Although the distance between the sting of the horned viper and the grave is no greater than a curt cry of pain and half a gasp, we children actually had the courage to grab one and pull it out of its hole, only to find it frozen solid like a dry branch. If you looked into its cold eyes, they would beseech you to return it to its hole. We would do as it wished, of course, when we felt a shiver run through its body, and we would replace it gently, for if we had dropped it, it would have smashed to pieces like a clay pot.

"Uburty was full of energy. With a smile on her face, she would come to gloat over the village's misfortune, ebullient like an impending flood. She would visit the houses at noon on fact-finding missions to make sure that no man had kept his virility and was doing what men like to do. She would enter laughing, wearing the most expensive and sumptuous clothes, with her glittering gold and her soft Moroccan slippers, teasing them with her pungent perfumes. This was what eventually convinced the village that she was using magic, for all she had inherited was a few scraps of land and a solitary palm tree. Her first husband, whom she had killed, left all his land and his palms to his children and didn't give her even a dried-up twig. Her second husband spent all the income from his palms on his bed in the internal medicine wing at Aswan Infirmary, whose balcony looked out over the first cataract. So great was her nerve that she felt no shame visiting houses at noontime when the men were in the fields lighting fires under the trees. She asked all the women if the spermatic drought still continued, and laughed and tried to pretend to feel sorry for them. They knew that she was enjoying their misfortune, but so far it had not occurred to a single woman that Uburty was a witch, and that she was the reason for the Almighty's wrath upon them.

"Uburty was flabbergasted when Bahiya, with her child at her breast, told her that her husband Karmy had managed it the previous night. Uburty was furious, her ugly tooth shook and her eyes turned yellow. She mounted her mule, and beating him with all her might, she rushed back to her enchanted house. For the first time, she summoned Kakoky during the day.

"With her weakening eyesight, she was unable to discern the ball of fire until it was upon her, and had taken the form of the revolting demon. His bellowing laughter also seemed to echo less in her ears.

"'Ho ho ho ho. Zeinab Uburty, you are a fool. Bahiya is not telling the truth. She suspects you, you idiot. Rest assured. None of those women will taste what you are deprived of, as long as you follow me. Rest assured, woman uglier than a mountain monkey. Ho ho ho.'

"Uburty was convinced, but two things still worried her. The first was whether Bahiya would discover her secret.

"'Ho ho ho. Bahiya will not discover your secret, rest assured.'

"The second thing was that she was becoming increasingly worried about the demon's impolite manner. His mockery grew worse day by day. He had forgotten the humility and submissiveness he had shown toward her previously, and now spoke to her with contempt. And this day he had compared her to a monkey. She was even more perturbed because she had never actually seen a monkey in her life and didn't know whether this thing called a monkey was uglier than her or not. If it was, then Kakoky had certainly insulted her. And when she confided to him the doubts that raged in her breast, he laughed once more that laugh that so unnerved her.

"'Ho ho ho. Eeeeh Uburty, Uburty. I have given you much. Clothes from the finest linen in the Egyptian Delta, and furs from the frozen lands of the north, the sweetest perfumes of Arabia, gold finer than the gold of the Incas, more wondrous in form than the ornaments of the pharaohs, and Moroccan slippers that not even your father dreamed of. I built you a house that the people of your land consider a miracle, and I filled it with soft butter and milk and honey and dates and apples from the Levant, whose breezes your grandfathers never even sniffed. Don't I have the right to mock you a little? Don't prevent me from mocking you, Uburty, or from smiling. Now tell me, why are you so sad? What do you lack, woman?'

"'In order to be a woman I need a man.'

"'And your husband?'

"'Colder than cold water in a stone jar at dawn.'

"'Ho ho ho.'

"'I hate your laugh.'

"'Ho ho ho.'

"'Give Infirmary the strength to be a man.'

"The demon turned into phosphorous gas then contracted into a ball of fire.

"'Ho ho ho. Ask the one who created him to do that, foolish woman.'

"Bahiya neglected her baby for a moment and it slipped out of its bundle. When she returned, she found it frozen solid. The women came to offer their condolences to the bereaved mother. They gathered around her with much chattering of teeth, and raising of eyebrows, and assorted contortions of the face, as well as meaningful and relevant sequences from the dance of the wailing women.

"The women sat in the narrow room around two braziers in which were blazing fires of dried corn husks. The affliction that had descended upon the village had now touched them directly. As they wondered about the reason, the fire and the closeness of their bodies together warmed them up. They began to recount the strange happenings, until the conversation, which contained hardly any chattering of teeth, came round to Uburty. She had taken her leave of them a short while before, and had continued to gloat even while paying her last respects to the tiny child of her cousin's daughter. They spoke again of her strange-looking house, which had been built in a single day by those strange, exotic-looking men who had never even set foot in the village, and whose presence Uburty had been unable to explain to the tribe. They talked about the sudden and abundant wealth, her gold and silver, and her valuable leather clothing. Some of them swore that Uburty's eyes had begun to take on a vertical appearance, just like the eyes of the demons among the people of the current. Bahiya took out her hand from under her shawl and waved it about nervously.

"'God curse Uburty. She's a witch.'

"They were silent for a while.

"'A witch?'

"'A witch!'

"'Immmmmm. How can she be a witch when she's more stupid than a cow?'

"Bahiya took out her left hand as well, beat the two of them on the top of her head, and let out a great scream.

"'Wayy wayy wayy wayy!'

"'Bahiya, we share your grief at the loss of your baby.'

"'I'm not wailing about my baby. I've just remembered something strange about Uburty's mother. I remember her one day talking about a hidden book of magic.'

"'May they both be cursed.'

"'And don't forget that her great-grandfather was Hamreen, the evil magician.'

"'Ibibibibib.'

"'And Uburty can just about read.'

"'Ahaah.'

"'So we know how her house was built and where the gold came from.'

"'And the clothes . . . and the rare leathers.'

"'And the slippers!'

"'And the mule!'

"'She's brought God's wrath upon us.'

"'The witch, she's put a spell on our men.'

"'Because all her life she's been without a real man.'

"'So what should we do, sisters?'

"'We'll have to tell the idiots.'

"'Indeed, we must tell the men.'

"'Come on then.'

"'Let's go.'

"The entire village was packed into the omda's spacious house. Even we children were there outside the house, jumping up and down to keep warm in the cold late afternoon. Everyone was desperate to see an end to the matter. There was much hustle and bustle and many shouts and curses. They could not reach an agreement. Should they kill her, or send her into exile? And if they killed her, how should they do it? Burn her? Hang her? Drown her? Or slaughter her with a sickle? When the old omda opposed this idea, for fear of the Turkish governor who was based in the town of Aneeba, the watchman, the barber, and Karmy were all furious. They were supported by the young men whose marriages had been postponed because of the crisis. Eventually, the men split into two camps. On one side, those in the pride of their manhood, and the ones who were just ready to marry, led by the chief watchman, and behind them all the women. On the other side were the older men and the merchants and notables led by the omda, the village grocer, and the wealthiest villagers. They included Selimto, who owned the boats that plied their trade between the villages. The latter group were worried about the repercussions the whole thing would have on their businesses. In the end, the foolhardy ones lined up behind the chief watchman and marched out of the court-yard of the omda's house. Sparks flew from their eyes, and even warmed them up a little and stopped their teeth from chattering. The women's ululations bolstered their enthu-siasm and gave them extra strength. What do you expect? The women were desperate for the spell to be lifted. The watchman carried his long rifle, Karmy had his hoe, and Abd al-Aal brought out his cutthroat razor. The others carried an assortment of whips, sickles, and clubs. They made a fine sight, a detachment ready for action. We ran behind them through the lanes of the village with the women, who were still ululating and singing songs of encouragement.

"As soon as we were outside the village, the fire of their enthusiasm began to wane. One man after another left the column, and then one woman after another, until it was no longer as fine a sight as it had been. There was a simple reason for this. They were afraid that they might be called as witnesses, and that the hypocritical omda would send them to the cruel governor. You've no idea how cruel he was. Evening was beginning to fall, and the bright light of day faded into grayness. The column, which now contained no more than ten men, headed up toward Uburty's hill. Even the ten began to slow down, except for Temple Door. He was enamored of his own tall, broad stature, was lusting after his latest two wives, and was keen to avenge the insults he had taken from the oldest one. And so, as he approached the bewitched house, he found himself all alone. The rest of the column was some way behind him. The rest of the villagers, including us young ones, were standing behind the last house, watching from afar. The first thing we heard were the screams of the chief watch-man and his calls for help. Well, I tell you, do you think anyone was willing to take a risk like that? Anyway, we saw him racing back down the hill, his turban flapping about his head. He was holding his rifle by the strap, dragging it over the sand behind him. He fell and stood up again and lost his shoes. At last he reached the ten men, who, though braver than the rest, were nevertheless nailed to the spot out of terror, and he fell to the ground unconscious.

"Back in his house, with his three wives and most of the village gathered around, and a fire blazing in the brazier, the effects of the cold and terror began to disappear. His strength returned, and he looked around him and relaxed when he realized that he was no longer in the witch's house.

"'I had almost reached Uburty's infernal house when, all at once, I saw it as a great fortress, taller and stronger than the castle of Ibreem. The door opened and I moved nearer. Suddenly two hideous wolves rushed out at me, snarling. The wall of the house was a mass of writhing, hissing snakes, and darting tongues over a yard long slid out of their mouths toward me. But the scorpions were worse than all of them put together. Dozens of them appeared out of the sandy ground, each as big as a large dog, and they grew taller till they came up to my thigh. They were buzzing. Did any of you ever know that scorpions buzzed? It was a buzzing that tore at my ears. So that's why you must forgive me for turning my back and running. I saw giant men on the roof, like the ones who built the evil house in the first place. Their bodies shone like dark mirrors. They had long swords and spears taller than palm trees, which they hurled at me. The wolves attacked, and snakes and scorpions were all around me. I fled. Me. The chief watchman. I can wrestle mountain wolves with my bare hands, and I fled. It was terrifying. God curse that woman and her evil magic.'

"He fainted again.

"Shame and fear hung over the village, weighing on it like the bitter cold. No one dared set foot anywhere near Uburty's hill.

"Uburty saw what happened. She wept and slapped her scrawny cheeks and tore out great clumps of her frizzy hair. She wept like she had never wept before. They had discovered her secret. Even though the watchman had suffered a humiliating defeat, there were several things that terrified her now: the villagers, the thought that the evil demon Kakoky might desert her and leave her unprotected, and that those loathsome creatures that had attacked the watchman would seize upon her and tear her to pieces.

"She locked herself in the house. For two long nights she didn't summon the wicked Kakoky. She wept and cursed him, and neither ate nor slept. On the third night she summoned him. The ball of fire came from amid the high peaks of Wawaat. She didn't see him until he assumed his devilish form in front of her. He laughed mockingly, pleased with what had happened.

"'Ho ho ho ho.'

"'You evil thing. Where are your promises? Where are your agreements? You haven't been any use to me at all.'

"'Uburty! Have you forgotten the food, drink, clothes, precious jewels, and house?'

"'Why do you remind me of them every time? What am I going to do? What a wretched mess I'm in. I haven't seen a single happy day while I've been with you.'

"'That's what you women are like. Always denying things. Uburty, stop all this women's nonsense!'

"'What did you do to my cousin's son? Did I ask you to do that?'

"'I was protecting you, and teaching him a lesson. Now the village is really afraid of you.'

"'I want their love.'

"'Whose love? Those who deprived you of ever having a man?'

"'I was content with my lot.'

"'Ho ho ho. You say that now. You should have thought about it before.'

"'I think it's time we went our separate ways.'

"'Entering the toilet is not like leaving it, Uburty. There is a pact between us. I bind all the men of the village for you, and in return I take your soul. You were the one who began with me, and I am the one who will finish with you. I am not a beast to be ridden upon by a foolish and capricious woman like you, Uburty. I am not your grandfather's servant.'

"'Are you no longer at my command, Kakoky? You used to kiss my feet and swear by your uncle, Iblees, that you would be my slave for life. Now you are rebellious. I will not have it. I will burn the pact, and with grandfather Hamreen's book I will imprison you in a bottle and torment you.'

"'Ho ho ho. You can never do that. You are a feeble-minded old woman, and I am Kakoky. With my infernal power, I have sucked up all your strength these last two months. My fire has dimmed the light of your eyes, and I have clouded the clarity of your perception. You won't be able to control me, Uburty. You'll never be able to read the book again after today, you stupid woman.'

"'I'll tear up the contract.'

"'Not until I say so, you old hag. Ho ho ho ho.'

"After the watchman's defeat, no one in the village did anything against Uburty. They were gripped with fear. They fought among themselves instead. Every hour a fight would break out. Everyone was against somebody. The demon had sown seeds of hatred and mistrust among us. Ever since those days the young haven't respected the old, and the old haven't been lenient with the young. We became like islands that never met, and if they did meet they exchanged blows and curses and withdrew inside their spikes like hedgehogs. There were lots of divorces and not a single marriage, many deaths and not a single conception. We heard for the first time of a son hitting his mother and father, of a daughter ignoring her parents, of a brother abandoning his own flesh and blood, and of a mother smothering her child.

"And then, on top of all that, imagine the anguish that struck us when we saw the mainstay of our lives, the palm trees, begin to change color; a cold blue mingling with the green, and reaching even the yellow tassels on the leaves. Almighty God preserve us. It was enough that our crops had died, and some of our animals and children. We had put up with everything, even the disappearance of the sun and the bitter cold, but we would never be able to bear the death of the palm trees.

"That was the evil weather that Amsheer brought, and it did not leave us until we too began to acquire a deathly blue color. We said to ourselves, 'Another week and we'll be dying by the dozen like the grasshoppers and the cock-roaches and the frogs.' But thanks be to God, Baramhaat came and we began to warm up. The palms regained their full greenness, and the swarthiness returned to our faces. One thing that didn't change, though, were the foolish quarrels between people. In the middle of Baramhaat the women began to remove some of the layers of clothing that they had wrapped around their bodies to keep warm, and to raise the question of their original problem with the men. Indeed, for that is what women are like, my children. The battles increased as the weather became more pleasant, and we were incapable of taking advantage of the change in the weather to confront the evil that was upon us. Barmouda came and took us by surprise with its scorching torrid heat, and the sun poured down endless blazing rays that burnt our skin. As it rose it was like a brilliant red disk the size of a mountain, a mass of fire amid a halo of copper flame. It would collide with the eastern mountains over there. Look toward the southeast, where there is a peak in the mountains the shape of a huge crescent lying on its back. In our day, the sun rose from over there. Its halo would crash into the rock and force its way through, and the summit has had that shape ever since. The crash would cause a great tremor, and every sunrise the earth would shake. Then the sun would cross the sky over the village like a mighty, incandescent ship. We could hear its fire hissing infuriatingly, and we were almost at the point where we could take no more. The animals became a little crazy and tried to thrust their heads under the sand to escape from the dread of the heat that crouched above them. The birds flew away, and the reptiles and insects retreated under boulders or to cracks in the mountains. Even our houses were damaged; some walls and the top half of the minaret, with its rusty copper crescent, collapsed.

"At the beginning of every day we had to wrap our eyes in a strip of dark cloth to protect them from the terrible glare of the sun, and the heat that diffused from the mountains, and the blinding light reflected off the ocean of sand and the surface of the Nile. The women let down their black veils over their faces, and the men let down the ends of their turbans. Before Barmouda was even half over, we had to cover the animals' eyes as well when we noticed they were inflamed and full of dust.

"The day, which had passed so slowly in the months of cold, now raced past with devilish speed. There were no more than two hours of daylight. No sooner had the sun reached the west and knocked the summit of Wawaat, than it was crashing up through the eastern mountains. Night was never longer than an hour and a half. Our bodies were confused and our nerves were in shreds. And we were no longer able to determine the phases of the moon. It would race through the sky like a shining filly and then suddenly disappear. We didn't try to follow it. Our eyes were too weak and tired.

"Uburty no longer showed herself. We no longer heard the brisk trot of her mule. Only the wretched raven came to perch on the gates of our houses and screech. Sometimes, during the hour and a half of night, we imagined we heard her voice in the distance, weak and tremulous, as if she were screaming at some creature that was in conversation with her, though we never once heard the speech of the creature.

"The soles of our feet, as you well know, are as hard as stone, but in those days it was impossible to walk a single step barefoot on the red hot sand, or on the rock, which had almost melted into volcanic lava. Any creature that touched the rock would leap into the air as if it had been struck by a thunderbolt. And when wisps of blue smoke rose from under stones and from between fissures in the rock, we would know that a scorpion or a snake or a lizard or a beetle was being roasted alive inside. Mount Wawaat was so hot that it seemed like a blazing sun come to rest on the earth. Its yellowness reflected the light so that none of us could look at it for longer than a second, not even with the aid of the ends of turbans and veils. In the middle of the day, as we hid from the heat in the shade, we could hear a bubbling sound fill the universe. It was bubbles boiling in the air, especially around the massive mountain. The trees on the edge of the village nearest the mountain were completely burnt and stood like columns of charcoal set in the ground, saying to whoever looked at them, 'Honestly, I used to be a green tree.'

"The animals became accustomed to the sun passing so low, and abandoned their madness after some of them died from ramming their heads into walls and rocks and trees.

"We slept under the arbors next to the clay water jars that were filled every sunrise and sunset. We would lie far apart, half-naked. There was no shame or embarrassment. After all, who could bear more than a light shirt on their body to protect them from the burning arrows of the sun and the heat of Wawaat that searched us out wherever we were and scorched us, even in the shade. Suckling babies could not stand the touch of their mothers' skin. Poor things. They cried constantly from the heat. If any mother wanted to feed her child, she would lay him on his back, take out her breast and, supporting her body on all fours, lean over him without touching him. That way her nipple would just reach his mouth and he would suck the milk as his mother's sweat poured down on him like bitter rain. Do you remember blind Hassan who died two floods ago? The reason he lost his sight was because he was a suckling child in those days and during the feeding his mother's burning sweat poured into his eyes and blinded him. Most of the babies died during that month. Anyway . . .

"One week into Barmouda we all left the village and went down to the bank of the Nile. We erected trellises and arbors under the palms, and we took our water jars and our belongings and set up permanent camp by the river, longing for its cool breeze, which had disappeared. But at least we had distanced ourselves a little from Mount Wawaat. The eastern mountains protected us from the sunrise until the sun came crashing over the peaks with a terrible sound. We moved back as we watched, for fear that we would be hit by flying rocks. Our mothers shielded us between their bodies or lifted us into the boughs of the huge sycamores to protect us from the flying splinters of rock. Our hearts trembled at the fearsome boom that the sun made when it scraped over the mountain top. We saw flaming red boulders roll down the mountainside and plunge into the wide river, which screamed in pain *tish sh sh* and the fish fled *sh sh sh sh tish tish tish tish* into the depths of the water to escape the intensity of the heat.

"The wild animals came down from the mountain. All of them: wolves, hyenas, and jackals; snakes, scorpions, and lizards. They settled by a ford just to the north of us where they crouched languidly, panting in silence. We paid no attention to them, and they were unconcerned with us. But our poor beasts were overcome by fear and would only sleep with us around them. From that day, they began seriously to contemplate the idea of committing suicide in order to be rid of the torment and the terror. We did not fear the wild beasts, for they were suffering the same tribulation as us. The heat scorched them and deadened their appetites for food and altercation, for even though they were all gathered in one place, not a single fight broke out between them, unlike us. We did suffer from rats though. They attacked us and got up to all sorts of mischief. Can you see my little finger? It's missing a knuckle. It was nibbled off by a huge rat the size of a cat.

"Dozens of conferences were held to discuss ways of making war on Uburty, now that we were certain that she was the reason for the wrath of the elements against us, and particularly because a new and more serious catastrophe was about to happen: the anger of the river, the anger of the mighty Nile. We had noticed with troubled hearts that the water was receding farther each day, leaving an ever greater distance of mud between its dwindling flow and the original banks. It became as emaciated as one of the shallow irrigation canals of the north. Selimto's boats were wooden shapes set in the mud and turned yellow in the fiery sun. The specter of drought was the final straw. We would surely lose our crops in the following season. We would go hungry and face shame and humiliation. The young children would continue to die, and the world would lose much of its stock of Nubians.

"There was no peace of mind whatsoever for Uburty. She was plunged into her darkest days and suffered greater torment than us. Kakoky came to her without her summoning him. He mocked her and her weakened eyesight. Food piled up in the house, but the devil knew she had lost her appetite with the worry and the grief and the dwindling supply of water in the clay jars, for he no longer filled them for her. She was tormented by thirst and the blazing heat. None of the fans in the house was working, due to some evil spell wrought by the demon. When she had the idea to mount her mule and ride down to the river to drink and fetch water, she found, as she tried to get on its back, that it would laugh and disappear. The old hag had to drink from the dishes that were placed under the jars, where the drops of water that seeped through them gathered and mixed with sand and dust. Both Kakoky and her loneliness were torturing her. She had lost the company of the adamir, and had taken upon herself the curse of those who deal with the people of the current. She wished Infirmary, whose absence this time had been longer than usual, would return. She longed for him to come back to her so she could rub his feet and look after him. She promised herself that she would never again beat him or insult him. In fact, she would let him beat her. She longed for the company of another human being. The treacherous, desperate woman did not know that he had left the infirmary for ever, having been transferred to Aswan cemetery, freed at last from the pains of his illness and the misery of his marriage to her.

"Uburty begged and beseeched Kakoky to make the mule obey her, so that she could escape from the village altogether. He refused, because none of the clauses in the contract contained such nonsense. Uburty exploded into a rage and hurled a leg of lamb that was by her side at the demon. It passed through his fiery body and landed on the floor behind him. She cursed him and reminded him of his inevitable end in the fires of Hell. He gave a raucous laugh of delight just to annoy her. 'Ho ho ho ho. We'll burn together, you evil, wicked woman, together with your grandfather Hamreen, who broke the barrier and came to me, just as you did, and whom I deceived, just as I will deceive those who come after you. We'll all burn together in Hell. Ho ho ho ho.'

"We were on the barren, mangy river bank, quarreling and hitting one another. We were consumed with despair. Our animals died, and some of those whose faith was feeble galloped into the river to drown themselves. We couldn't rescue them, and we left them to wallow and sink in the strip of slimy mud with dozens of dead rats all around them. A rotten suffocating stench filled the air like a pall.

"Uburty became almost completely blind. The sun still scraped against the peaks of Wawaat as it set, and the tremors of sunset still shook the earth. But despite the thunderous noise and the flying rocks, the thirst that burned her throat and body forced her to go down to the river. Her head was bare and she hadn't had a bath for a

77

month. She emitted a powerful stench. On her way Kakoky appeared to her once again, assuming his favorite shape, a screeching raven announcing her death. A dog leapt about her and laughed. She smelled a clay jar of cold water but couldn't see it, then the smell vanished. She knew these were Kakoky's tricks, but she couldn't even move her wooden tongue to curse him. She passed through the deserted houses of the village down into the valley bottom, which had been lush and fertile before she destroyed it. She trampled over the dry straw. On her way to the camp, she crawled on all fours so as not to be seen. The place was in total darkness and no one was going to notice the likes of her. Uburty used her ears to make her way along. Luck befriended her, and a woman fell over her.

"'Bismillah! Who are you?'

"Uburty didn't answer. Kakoky had taken all her clothes and gold and silver, and she was no longer recognizable. She drew her face toward that of the woman until their noses touched. It was Bahiya. Uburty smiled at her hopefully.

"'Bahiya. It's me, your aunt. Have mercy upon me.'

"Bahiya was horrified. She leapt to her feet and pulled herself together.

"'You'll get no mercy from me, you old witch, you grand-daughter of witches. May you be cursed in this world and the next. You caused all our troubles. You caused the death of my son.'

"Filled with hatred, she grabbed Uburty's frizzy hair. Uburty howled and begged for mercy as her body swung left and right like a pendulum. Finally, Bahiya flung her violently to one side with a strength she did not know she possessed. Uburty's skinny body flew through the air and crashed into the wall of a bamboo cote. The cote collapsed and the roof fell on top of her. The noise of the collapsing cote and Uburty's screams unnerved the wild animals, and they stood up and snarled. From where she lay, Uburty could make out the shapes of people gathering. She heard their curses and their muttering, and the sound of dry grass and reeds breaking under their feet. She knew they would kill her, so she turned and ran, heading north. She ran into trees and fell flat on her face more than once. Each time, she stood up, panting like a dog. She approached the ford where the wild beasts lay. Their nervousness increased, as they heard the screams of Uburty and the cries of the people in pursuit. The snakes raised themselves up and drew back their heads in readiness to strike. The scorpions unfurled their stings, though they well knew that their poison had solidified. All of the wild beasts, whether they were on the bank or on the dry mud by the bank, even those squatting in the mud that was still slimy, stood up and turned their heads toward the furiously advancing adamir. The pursuers stopped. They let Uburty slip from their hands. Uburty continued running and panting and falling and dragging herself to her feet until she was among the wild beasts. She tripped over a wolf and landed by the jaw of a hyena, who took one look at her and turned away his face in disgust. The beasts lay down again and the poisonous insects returned to their languid inactivity. They were all panting from the killer heat and lay just a few paces apart from one another.

"Uburty was right in the middle of them, but neither the beasts nor the insects paid her the slightest attention. The horrendous weather and the scorching heat stifled their appetite for food, both during the day and at night, and exhaustion had drained them of any desire to hunt prey. You'd have thought they were dogs or cats. For a few moments, Uburty spluttered and gulped great drafts of air. Then she sniffed the emaciated water course. She headed toward it, following her nose. She stumbled and rolled down onto the dry mud. Her body came to rest against a wolf. She cursed it and pushed it away. It snarled and drew back. A few steps more and her legs sunk up to the knees in the oozing mud. She reached the slow-moving waters. She bent down and with her palms she lifted the water to her mouth and drank greedily. Inches away, she noticed two yellow eyes exuding a yellow phosphorescent glow. They moved toward her and with them came the jaws of a huge crocodile. Her mouth was at the water that lay gathered in her palms. She stopped drinking and let out a great scream before she fled. She fell in the mud and regained her feet. As she scrambled up the bank, she heard the crocodile's laughter. It was Kakoky. She rushed back to her hill in a state of shock with her scrawny body covered in mud up to her neck, which was now as thin as a stick.

"Temple Door was preaching a sermon hotter than the days themselves. He lambasted the men and the cowardice they had shown that day they deserted him in front of Uburty's house. The women fired up the men's zeal, convincing them that Uburty was no longer as powerful as she had been, which was proven by the courageous way Bahiya had dealt with her and the fact that she had stumbled half-blind upon the wild beasts. The beasts hadn't eaten her for the same reason they hadn't eaten the sheep and goats who wandered among them in the hope of finding final release from their suffering.

"Their flaming torches lit up the ends of the fleeting night. They armed themselves with their motley collection of weapons and swore that they would not fail a second time. They would burn down the infernal house with Uburty inside it and she would be an example to anyone with a mind to take heed.

"If Uburty had been able to take hold of the demon Kakoky, and if she had possessed enough strength and a few teeth instead of that one leaning tooth that prevented her from closing her mouth properly, she would have bitten him on the neck and sunk her fangs into his windpipe until he convulsed in pain like a slaughtered chicken, and she wouldn't have left him until his last breath rattled in his throat and he died. That is what she would have done if she had been able.

"She went into the house, yelling curses at him as she wandered through the high-walled rooms, which Kakoky had emptied of furnishings. She cursed him and her voice echoed metallically through the deserted house. She even reviled his satanic master, Iblees.

"'Where are you, you treacherous bastard? Show yourself to me so that I can spit in your face. You said Bahiya would never discover my secret, but she did. You lied to me. Damn you and your kind. Kakoky, you bastard, where are you?'

"She could smell him, and she knew he was there. But he was teasing her, and she didn't know that he had turned himself into a louse and was lying stretched out behind her ear, smiling.

"She rushed over to the ebony box and took out the contract, which was written on vellum in Kakoky's own hand. He had written it in her blood, which she had shed according to his request from a cut she made directly below her navel. It was signed by Kakoky, and by Uburty with the print of her left foot which she had smeared in her blood, and had been ratified with the seal of Iblees, which shone with weird spiral shapes. She looked for fire and she found it igniting spontaneously before her. She burned the parchment as she listened to Kakoky's laughter, but she was not afraid . . . until the contract was burned and the fire turned into Kakoky.

"'Ho ho ho ho. Uburty, you've burned the contract with your repulsive little hands. Your turn is over and I will leave you to your worldly fate. This is where we must part. I will miss you, my dear, and I must admit that you are a pleasant person, and I very much enjoyed your stupidity. Until we meet to burn together in Hell, farewell. Ho ho ho ho.'

"The second column, under the light of the torches, was moving out. It was almost dawn and northern breezes were blowing, though in their zeal they did not feel them. Then the flames started to flicker and the column stopped. They intoned God's name and shouted His praise, and then rushed on, feeling at last that the Creator was with them. They passed through the deserted village and on toward Uburty's hill. The shriveled old woman was calling from her hill as loud as she could though her voice was now no more than a hiss. 'I swear to God that I've repented. I regret what I've done. I've abandoned the ways of the Devil. You must believe me. I'm one of you after all, one of the tribe. I've repented.'

"'Ahaaaa. Now she's remembered repentance? Now that her strength has gone and her secret is out? Now that her sight has failed her and danger approaches? Now she repents? Immmmmm.'

"The torches approached the evil house. The high walls looked like phantoms. We were all there, even me. We weren't afraid. We were expecting wolves and snakes and scorpions that roared, and the giants that shone like dark mirrors, but nothing appeared. As soon as we got to the gate the whole house vanished. We stood there aghast. Uburty had fled up to Mount Wawaat seeking refuge there. It was to be her grave, as it had been her grandfather's. We returned to the river bank, having decided to continue the chase after the trauma of sunrise.

"We adamir stood by the bank, our faces turned toward the peaks of the eastern mountain, concentrating on the formidable summit that looked like a crescent lying on its back. The River People were in front of us in the dwindling stream that remained for them. They peered above the surface of the water looking at the edge of the eastern sky with their tails turned toward us and quivering with tense expectation. They were all hoping for an end to the torment, and that the burning furnace of the mountain would come crashing down upon them and put an end to the tragedy of their shrinking river, the Nile. The good ones had heads with gills, wide eyes, and tiny mouths which gently opened and closed, giving praise to the Almighty Creator. The evil ones had bulbous heads and narrow foreheads with even narrower eyes and repulsive mouths with razor-sharp fangs. Our animals stood among us, while the wild beasts crouched silently at their ford, their heads turned east. Behind us the different kinds of trees inclined their westward-facing branches slightly to the east to observe the decisive moment. Northern breezes began to blow, weak and limp. The mountain retained its dark hue, close to the color of heavy purple, as the first glimmers of light appeared in the sky. This was followed by a pale red glow behind the peaks of the mountain, which still shielded the sun from us, but whose dark complexion had lightened considerably. As the daylight increased and gained strength, our hearts beat faster. As the moment approached, the mothers of us children drew us back as a precaution. The roofs of the houses and the amputated minaret of the village mosque seemed like silent ghosts lying in wait. The red halo moved higher . . . higher . . . higher. Then the bright red face of the sun appeared and ascended, and the heat grew slowly fiercer. The redness of the sun and its halo poured down onto the summit of the mountain and turned its crags the color of blood. At last the haloed sun slipped out from behind the mountain, awesome and menacing. The disk alone was a league in circumference, and the halo many leagues. It was a solemn dreadful sight, that ball of fire, as it climbed into our sky humming and hissing in calm glory. From under their lids, our eyes observed it apprehensively.

"The first to relax were the River People. They thrashed the water with their fins and tails and made thousands of little fountains before returning to their abodes in the depths of the water. The wild beasts and insects of the mountain were overjoyed. They howled and roared and hissed in a harmonious chorus; then they went their separate ways, at first in groups and then each one alone, running and crawling back to the mountain. Our animals also understood before we did. They leapt about and ran around one another and us in circles. The trees returned to their natural position and those leaves that were still left on the branches danced furiously, even though the breeze was gentle. Our minds were not put at rest until we saw that the sun had passed the eastern mountain and was shining bright as silver over the Nile, and no harm had befallen us. We prostrated ourselves before the Most Merciful and gave thanks.

"The crash and tremor that normally happened at sunrise never came. Our mothers took us back to the men, and we all embraced one another, for it seemed as if our troubles were coming to an end. Nevertheless, we still had to finish what we had begun so that the wrath upon us would not return.

"The second column was truly imposing. Its sacred mission was to exterminate the source of the evil that had befallen all creatures. There were riders mounted on donkeys and four cameleers, as well as the infantry. Each man carried two water skins. They started looking for tracks on the hill. Although the sun was a little higher in the sky, it was still hot. The mountain responded to the heat of the sun with a heat of its own just as strong, and the column was besieged and pounded by waves of fire. In less than an hour, they were completely exhausted. Those on foot gulped down their two skins of water and had to pull out. The riders continued the search up and down the difficult heights of Wawaat. Before they had gone five leagues, the donkey riders returned, through no choice of their own. That was because under the influence of the boiling heat, the donkeys had decided to head for home.

"The sun quickly reached its zenith. The tracks disappeared and their eyes became blurred. They arrived at a point where the path diverged. They decided to split into two, with two camels following each path. They agreed to fire three shots if they found Uburty and to return home before sunset just in case the sun crashed into Wawaat, and they were caught under a shower of burning rocks and incinerated. The chief watchman was with Karmy. It was their good fortune to find Uburty and to witness her final end with their own eyes. The path they took led them to a vast depression like a lake of polished yellow sand, which glared excruciatingly, and they had to unwrap another fold of their turbans to protect their eyes. The camels were drooping, worn, and wilting with thirst. The two men couldn't see clearly because of the glare from the sand, and before another hour had passed their copious tears had soaked the layers of cloth over their eyes, and drenched their chins and run down over their chests. Suddenly, Karmy noticed a black rock like an island amid the sea of sand. They headed toward it. They were certain they had found the object of their quest when they noticed a pack of hyenas on their left moving in the same direction. As the men approached, the hyenas stopped and watched, desperate for a meal after long enforced hunger. The body was lying on its back. They dismounted from their camels and walked cautiously toward it asking the Almighty to protect them. It was Uburty. The sun had dried up her already wizened body till it looked like the brittle remains of one long passed away. Her face was pock-marked though she had never had the pox. Her mouth was completely shattered, with its leaning tooth still inside. Her eyes were open and a look of terror was in them. Bloody teardrops were still flowing and they made red patches on the sand by each ear. The men turned their faces away, and the camels snorted in fear. They looked around and saw a beast approaching from the far end of the sandy lake. Slowly and confidently, it came toward them without making a sound, as if it were swimming. They mounted their camels and moved away from the rock and the corpse. The hyenas lay motionless like stone effigies. The beast came nearer. It was like no beast they had ever seen, as high as a cow, dark and shiny in color. Its head was enormous even in proportion to its massive powerful body. Its eyes were wide, but they paid no attention to the camels or the men on the camels or the hyenas. Its sight was focused solely on its goal, the ill-fated corpse. When it reached her it raised its head and let out a chilling shriek that was not like the cackling of the hyena or the roar of the lion or the howl of the wolf. It was unlike the sound of any animal we know in our mountains. The camels started and pulled back, and the hyenas moved away. The corpse twitched and moaned and wept. The monster opened its mouth and a strange fire issued from between its terrifying jaws. Of its own accord Uburty's head rose a few inches off the sand and into the gaping jaws that tore it from the rest of her body. Uburty's skull shattered between the monstrous jaws and splinters of bone flew about inside the evil mouth. The beast raised its head back, as if it were sucking the brain from the skull, right down its gullet. Then it turned around and went back calmly and confidently in the direction it had come from. The hyenas pounced on the body and tore it to pieces, growling and snorting.

"The chief watchman and Karmy returned to their senses to feel a cool refreshing breeze. It was as if something from above was sucking up the air and taking all the dust in great gulps. The heat quickly became less intense. They were able to look upward, and they removed the edges of their turbans from over their eyes. The good old sun was ascending back to its normal position. They fired three shots into the air.

"That's what happened to Zeinab Uburty in the end. The same thing that happened to her wicked grandfather Hamreen. But we never did find the evil book and burn it. It remains hidden somewhere, waiting for a certain day. . . .

"I wonder if any of you young men will think someday about looking for it, in order to cross over to the other side and enter into a pact with the demon Kakoky."

The River People

S easons of the south, uninterrupted since the dawn of
time, beware of the deluge. It will engulf you for an
eternity in one final season . . . the season of grief.

On that day the villagers took out lamps and flaming
torches. They searched the mountains and the cultivated
strip of land along the edge of the river. There was no sign
of Asha. Korty, a child one year younger than her sister,
swore that Asha had not died. She had not been eaten by a
wolf. Her foot had not been lashed by the dark scorpion's
sting. She had not been bitten by the horned viper. In tears,
Korty insisted that her sister had gone to the River People,
where there are neither wolves, nor scorpions, nor snakes.
Korty wept and insisted, "Asha looked into the water and
went off. But she'll come back, she'll come back. She's
happy with them now, in bliss among people whose waters
know no end of joy; their tambourines are never silent;
they are untroubled by fear of a future that will drive them
away; their constant ululations surge with the perch dance
and never end."

I was still young. I waited till the fisherman wasn't looking, then I grabbed his laden basket and threw the poor fish back into the hamboul. The fisherman chased me, but his big pot belly slowed him down. I fled in fear through the stalks of corn. It wasn't the first time I'd rescued tormented fish from his basket prison. I ran up the hill toward the houses with the fisherman still behind me fuming and cursing. Just at the door of my grandmother, Anna Korty, he caught me. If it hadn't been for you, Siyam, he would have smashed my head against the mud bench by the wall. He grabbed my braided hair, and I screamed out in fright. In a flash you came rushing forward and bit his hand to make him let me go. I stepped back and watched the struggle between your slim figure and the fisherman. I yelled out, "Anna Korty . . . Anna Korty!" They managed to remove you from his grip. You were bloody and your eyes were swollen, and the fisherman was bleeding from his right side and his fat belly where your sharp teeth had been. Siyam, I fell even more deeply in love with you, and I wept in sympathy for your wounds. You were my companion deep in the thick fields of wheat and corn and out on the farky. And when we grew a little older, nothing could keep me apart from you, no word of admonition that we were too old to be playing together, nor the gossip of the old women who sit by the wall, nor the stern censure of my uncles . . . not even my father's violent slaps.

I respected my mother and father, who were worried about my beauty and the roving eyes of both the young and the old men. I had no one but my grandmother. I would sit by her side in the shade of her wall on the woven mat. She would wrap herself in her red shawl, even in summer, with her uncovered hair a mass of flame from the henna dye. She loved me and protected me from the wrath of my mother and father. She would say, "Asha, you look a lot like me, but the real resemblance is between you and my late sister Asha Ashry, the daughter of the Turkish governor. She was the most beautiful woman, combining the fair skin of our Turkish father with the dark hue of our mother, a daughter of the south, like a blend of milk and molasses. Asha. Her name was never spoken unless followed by the word 'ashry,' which means beautiful. She was a good girl, Asha Ashry, a dreamer, a flower of beauty. As soon as she was in her eighth spring, your age now, the women were asking after her for their sons. And by the time she was twelve the men were fighting over her. She wasn't even safe from the lustful looks of the elders. If it hadn't been for the influence of our father the governor and his serious position, an appointment from the north, the omda would have married her and set her as a rose among his succession of wives.

"Your grandmother Asha Ashry was madly in love with the River People. She used to love sitting on the bank, her gaze wandering over the smooth surface of the water. I would always hear her sharing her thoughts with them, and when I warned her about her infatuation with them, she would smile and say, 'Korty, my dear sister, don't be afraid. The River People are kind and peaceful. Korty, don't give my secret away.' And at dawn far from the eyes of the villagers she would take off her clothes, slip into the hamboul, and swim softly, laughing, her sweet body bobbing up and down with the gentle swell of the waves. She would head back to the bank and whisper in my ear, 'The sand at the bottom is soft and cool, unspoiled by the running of the wolf or the march of the scorpion or the crawling of the horned viper. Korty, one day the surface of the river will become translucent like a fine white sheet spread over the angareeb, and I will see the good things and the good folk hidden in its depths.'

"Our father the governor went away and didn't come back. Those northerners are cruel and inconsiderate people. Your grandmother wasn't even fully grown, but hungry eyes were on the prowl. Othman took her in his arms one day and convulsed against her tender body. The old men gathered in a final effort to restore order. A battle was about to break out between the families.

"It was torment for Asha when they locked her up in the house in compliance with the elders' ruling. They said she was disturbing the moral fiber of the village. Some fools had started telling tales about her. They stopped my sister from sitting on the bank of the river to look at the clear waters and whisper secrets to its people. They forbade her from filling the water jugs with the party of girls that went down to the river every morning and sunset. Asha Ashry suffocated between the walls. She had crying fits when she heard the women babbling about how she would be the cause of bloodshed in our otherwise untroubled village.

"They are at a wedding in the next village, across the farky. I nodded off and forgot about Asha Ashry. In the middle of the night they came back. She wasn't there. I woke up to their violent shakes and screams. She had disappeared into the night. Your grandmother Asha Ashry had disappeared.

"That's why, when your mother gave birth to you, the year they built the dam, and you came out to us, I cut your cord and shouted, 'Asha, Asha, Asha has returned." You're the exact image of her, so I called you Asha and the people of the village added the second name. Your name became the same as that of your grandmother: Asha Ashry. But beware, Ashry. Don't stick too close to the river. Don't wander along the bank at the time of the flood when the water gathers and flows into the farky. Don't go down there on your own."

Siyam, your father's house clung to the house of Anna Korty and my heart clung to yours. You were a few years older than me, and much taller. We grew up together, Siyam, like the palm tree lovers; two palm trees, a medium one leaning against a tall one, like a young woman resting her head on the chest of her tall, young man. I said the shorter one was me, Asha Ashry, and the tall one was you, Siyam. The two palm tree lovers . . . just like you and me.

And when the dam from the north fouled our valley you went away until your feet touched the waves of the salty sea.

In the farky there were rocks scattered everywhere, as if they had been thrown about at random, and some large boulders. At flood time after the dam was built, the water would flow over the farky and surround us. The scorpions and snakes fled in its wake, coming up to the villages from inside the mountains. Incidents of stinging and death from poisoning increased. As children, we went there time after time, you and I, and crossed the high stone bridge with the water all around us. I held on to your gallabiya, afraid of falling in. In the early summer, the water level fell and left the sand exposed. The sun ignited it, and it burned our bare feet. I jumped up and clung to your high shoulders. We would climb onto the rock and throw rough sand over the cracks, then rush down to see the sand slip through and watch the fine grains fall softly down. We moved the heavy boulders and looked underneath for scorpions. I screamed, pretending to be afraid, and moved back. The scorpion raised his poisonous tail and crawled about, terrified. You talked to him and moved your foot near his weapon. You lay on the floor and moved your head toward him menacingly, and I screamed with fright. Then, bravely, you killed him with a stone and took me back to the village. You were my heart's desire, my true love incarnated. Why did you go away?

"Saleh wants you," my mother said. "He's spoken to your father. Marry him."

"What do you think of Dahab?"

"Asha Ashry, young Mounib's ballads and the love poems he dedicates to you are in all the villages. They're singing them at their weddings and in the evenings when they stay up drinking cups of aragi. You're as stubborn as a Turk."

"What do you think about Yahya? Hassan then? Bakry . . . Zakariya . . . the omda's son?"

"Asha! You're trying my patience. Siyam has been away a long time. Your father and your uncles are saying that you'll bring us nothing but trouble."

How could I belong to any man other than Siyam, companion of my childhood and youth? Who else had I ever felt so comfortable with in all my life? I loved the smell of his sweat when he came back from the fields. The smell of aragi on his breath after his nights out enchanted me. How much I cried when his father beat him! Siyam, how handsome you looked riding your donkey with your feet almost touching the ground. You were so tall. At the crowded weddings I would watch you and rejoice as you moved with a hundred other dancers. The light from the lamps and torches shone on your chest above the curved hem of your white gallabiya, on your noble collar bone, your ebony face, and your high turban. You were far taller than the rest, as if you weren't one of them. Mounib never dared to sing his love songs until you had left. The omda's tall son never dared to show off his body until you, Siyam, the tallest of them all, left the floor.

Walking through the narrow, cultivated strip my soul peers out toward the sea, and sniffs its salty Alexandrian breeze. There Siyam is anchored, to the north of our dark mountain upon whose flanks the houses nestle. To my right is the somber Nile's wide hamboul, and beyond, the western mountains. One ridge has broken away and come to rest, smooth, like a plump round thigh, a few meters out into the water. I walk by its side. I can feel the eyes of the people watching me in dread. They whisper to one another,

"Siyam's gone away. He read the Fatiha for Asha Ashry, then he went away. He's forgotten her for the bright lights of the city in the north. Who could forget Asha Ashry, who brought together the beauty of the Turks and the Nubians, except a fool like Siyam. What a fool!"

Dam piled high, you are the same age as me. You split up lovers. They dumped you into the way of the mighty river. You have blocked the life-flow of water. Behind you it has built up and drowned half our land. The river is good like its people, but the dam confined the water in a huge lake. The water swelled up like boiling milk, and as it rose it swallowed up half the green valley and destroyed it. It drowned lines of palm trees and polluted the sweet water. It ruined the time of peace and purity. We moved out, leaving behind our cool spacious houses for cramped sweltering ones that hung on the side of the mountain like carbuncles. We crowded in on the scorpions, and they crowded in on us. We chased away the snakes, and they came back and surrounded us. The wolf's howl echoed deep in our ears: "Beware, you are too close to my territory." We drowned in the murky yellow of the mountain and our hearts longed for the bright yellow sand of our own land, for the higher sands were barren and brought forth neither a stalk of corn nor a clump of green. They bred only scorpions and kept the rattlesnakes and vipers warm.

We could no longer make a living. The men went north to work as servants, and around their waists they wore cummerbunds that were red like the faces of their English masters and the beys. They went north to the seaside girls, where the water is salty and does not quench the thirst. Siyam, I'm waiting for you. Our river is sweet. Their sea is salty. When will you realize that and come back? Our air is dry and clear, theirs cloudy and damp with rain. It will make your body soft and your soul heavy, and it will weigh on your eyelids and weaken your resolve. Has your resolve weakened, Siyam?

On Sheikh Shebeyka's birthday people came in droves, some riding donkeys and camels, crossing the sand, passing through hamlets and villages on their way to his shrine. I insisted we attend, and we went by boat floating with the current down the river of goodness. Opposite the temple of Abu Simbel, in front of the statues of the most beautiful of all women, our princess Nefertari, princess of the south, we clapped to the rhythm and sang of her beauty and of ours. We were happy. We sang songs in praise of the prophet and dreamt of a visit to his tomb. But at the four statues of Ramses, mighty conqueror from the North, we did not sing. We looked at him in silence and disapproval, and we smiled at the monkeys that climbed up his mountain.

On the hill in front of Sheikh Shebeyka's mausoleum, we complained to him of our confusion amid sighs of despair, and we muttered nervously our fears of the future.

On the way home, the north wind filled the white sail and carried us back upstream.

Siyam, you used to race the other boys across the river. You were always the first to reach the west bank where the mountain came to rest its massive thigh in the hamboul. You would climb up the smooth granite. The rest all arrived after you, yelling songs from the tale of Fana, the maiden, at the tops of their voices. Then they would listen to the songs echo in the throat of the western mountains, and the surface of the river would move restlessly. "Fana, what did they feed you on . . . butter or milk?"

But you didn't sing about the tale of Fana. You sang in your loud voice, "Asha, what did they feed you on . . . butter or milk?"

Your passion and the laughter of the boys echoed through the air. I was overjoyed that you had declared your love. My father and uncles were angry. They cursed you and your father. The old folk said, "It's bad manners, announcing a girl's name. It's bad manners. It's a sign. The age of true principles is passing. It's the beginning of a twisted time. No one knows what sadness and worry it will bring save our Lord God, the Ever Mindful."

My father and my uncles have been accusing Anna Korty of encouraging me to wait for you. They are afraid of what the men might do to me . . . and the gossip. They sense fear from the river. If they had been able to keep me locked up in the house, they would have done so years ago. Simple Saleh went away with you, and he comes back every winter. He desperately wants me. Mounib has told the whole bank about his love. Standing by his shadoof, he sings ballads about me. The girls say the shadoof has started moaning, and the moans blend with the ballads like the wings of a bird circling in the east, hovering in the sky above the high villages.

They all want me and I am waiting for you, Siyam. When will you come back?

The first signs of the flood, reddish brown, swam adamantly over the land. The fish leapt about in wild abandon and some landed in the shallows where they writhed and suffocated. Most of them were perch. I loved them. I went to where one lay, looking at me with lidless eyes, his delicious mouth agape, and I kissed him and threw him back into the hamboul. Everyone laughed at me. "Asha Ashry is in love with the fish and the River People," they said. The fools wouldn't understand the lesson. They didn't learn anything from what happened to the fisherman. The River People punished him. He had a daughter with a harelip.

The flood stretched out over the narrow valley and covered it, confining us to our houses hanging from the side of the mountain. There was nothing for us to do except till small narrow plots around the houses and plant vegetables. Sometimes the water reached even these consumptive scraps of land and swallowed them up, bit by bit. Our only job then was meeting the men who had migrated, when the season of their return came around. Then everyone would be together again, and the weddings would start.

The weddings come one after the other. At night, the villages are lit up with lamps and torches. Double-barreled shotguns are fired into the air. The men have the fire of aragi in their veins. They beat the tambourines and clap and stamp the ground with their feet in proud rhythmic steps. The virgins' hearts are aflutter, and their very cells dance to the flood of hot southern songs.

Inside the circle of women, I dance the perch dance: fast, flirtatious steps, both arms outstretched, one in front, one behind. The men can't take their eyes off me, and the girls are delighted. They approve since I am above competition and beyond the reach of their fiery, jealous tongues. I am Asha Ashry . . . beauty and dance: the beauty is a double gift from the loins of the Turkish governor and the belly of Nefertari, princess of the south. The dance is a gift from the River People, from the perch, who taught me how to dance their dance the correct way.

Before the dam, the yearly flood came slowly, pouring gently into the sprawling water course. Brown goodness with a touch of red, full of fertile silt, seeping into the life-giving earth. The valley conceived and brought forth billions of tiny green shoots that broke up through the surface to flower under the sun, and grow into fine green plants, a feast for the hungry folk to behold. No one went away then.

Ah, Siyam, every night there is a wedding, yet my heart is sad. Every night a procession escorting the bride to the groom's house, with the women and girls in rows behind the men, sprinkling salt, rose water, and Daughter of Sudan perfume. They sing in their soft, delicate voices:

To the Prophet we give praise
The lover of the Prophet we praise
We give praise and ask protection.

Siyam, you're so forgetful. Five times the water has flooded the land and passed into the farky, separating the hamlets and turning them into islands. Five wedding seasons and the men carry each groom, and each groom waves his sword in the air, and the men sing to him:

Raise up, O groom, your sword for your guests.

The tambourines pound and hands clap to the beat. The ground shudders to the pulsating rhythm of arrogant feet, and the women's ululations reverberate through the night's festivities like brass strings.

You are forgetful, Siyam. As a boy you took my grandfather's sword from above my grandmother's bed. You said you would dance with that burnished sword on the night of the henna, and that you would tie a dagger to your arm on our wedding night and crack your long whip and no friendly rival's whip would touch you. Strong and tall like a palm tree, you would close the door behind us and not one of the lads would dare climb on the roof to steal a look at us. And I would say to you, "The following morning we will bathe in the river, a purification, so that God will kindly bless us and grant us children." You have forgotten, Siyam. The River People are asking me about you. What am I supposed to say?

Winter went and came back. Several times it went and came back. Simple Saleh married Nafisa. Mounib's shadoof grew weary of the string of desperate ballads, and he got married. There was nothing left for me except the wailing of the shadoof.

The omda's son went to the north. He disappeared. News arrived that he had married a girl from by the sea. His mother slapped her cheeks with grief for the loss of her son. She was hiding her shame from the women and her embarrassment from her sister and her sister's daughter, who had been waiting for him. The omda was greatly saddened. His head hung low. Whenever the men offered their condolences, he would croak, "My son's dead and I will accept no solace."

Thank God, you are not like the omda's son. Your annual letters still arrive. You say you will come, but you never do.

I have been watching the mail boat for years, a white goose with her beak sticking out of her back. I wonder how, when she's white, she belches out blackness?

Inside the circle of the perch dance, girls younger than me are already tired. I dance with the mothers. I am the perch princess. A girl almost ten years old appears out of the crowd and faces me boldly to dance. I smile at her. It is the daughter of Simple Saleh and Nafisa. "You've grown, Fatim Nafisa. You've entered the perch's circle." A new generation is looking forward to its destiny. And I can feel a tired numbness moving up my legs and a great, dry emptiness growing inside me. Come on, Fatim, I'll teach you the rules of the perch dance. This is the turn, the winding movement, the affected shyness in the poise of the neck, and the tilt of your head, your arms outstretched in front and behind. Straighten your back. Hide half of your face with your maiden's veil, then uncover it. Move toward the sea of eager men, as if you're going to drown in them, and then slip away and let them lick their lips. Clever girl! Don't be too suggestive, for that's thought distasteful and brings gossip. You will learn, Simple Saleh's daughter. I catch the eyes of her mother Nafisa as she dances in the rows of women around the circle. On her forehead is the disk of the Almighty, for she is married, and only married women wear the disk of the Almighty. Her eyes are content, proud of her daughter. You are lucky, Nafisa. You have Saleh, even if he is simple and his father was simple before him. A man who can quench your thirst, and who gave you Fatim and made your heart smile. The bride sings:

To the Prophet we give praise
The lover of the Prophet we praise
We give praise and ask protection.

No one dares walk along the bank of the river before dawn, unless they have a heart of stone. My heart is like white milk, but I still walk along the bank. I while away the time playing with the water and the River People. I am not afraid of the demon on dry land, and I do not fear the genie of the water. I am under the protection of the perch, the protection of the River People. Forgetful Siyam has been away a long time. Anna Korty has grown old and leans on a wooden stick. Who do I have left except you, People of the River? Siyam is a fool. He works in a mansion by the sea and has a Greek girlfriend. They say she's a children's nanny. She doesn't know the meaning of the word shame. Siyam drinks alcohol like the beys and the foreigners, and then staggers about and falls into bed with the Greek girl. Siyam, you don't fast. You went north, beyond the cursed dam and beyond the cataract until you alighted by the sea and sipped its salty water. Siyam, you went away and left the fasting to me.

A small child, only a babe in arms, fell into the well, and the guardian at the bottom touched his mind. He became known as Klow To, the Well Child, and was ever after slightly unhinged. Squint-eyed, he rode a stick that he pretended was a donkey, and with his gaping mouth he would make predictions. He would find a piece of paper and give it to whoever was going to receive a letter. He would hand a stone to a woman, and she would get a parcel full of gifts from her husband or a son who had migrated north. He would speak mysterious words, and then time would bring them to pass.

Klow To gave my friends paper and stones and spoke to them. To one he said, "Your blood will flow," and in the winter she got married and her blood flowed. And to another, he announced, "Your belly is big," and she became pregnant, and her belly swelled out. Every time he gave one of them the good news, he would look greedily at her chest. She would lean toward him, and he would put his hand down the top of her gallabiya and fondle her breasts as a treat for his auspicious prediction. The girls laughed and Klow To trotted off on his stick donkey. All my friends had good news from him, even the young girls, and their breasts were fondled. They married and brought forth the fruit of their wombs. But Klow To never gave me any good news. All he did was stare with his squint eyes, longing to grab my breasts.

I sit by the river. The sacred Nile flows unceasingly like an endless dream. Fine delicate whirlpools are on the surface of the water like the generous dimples on the plump bronzed body of a girl sauntering shyly along. All around our Nile is a translucent halo, and the tips of the waves are gentle like the steps of a tender young child. Its perfumed breeze diffuses throughout the universe, and I take in great drafts through my nose, my eyes, my pores. Our mountains and the sky before sunrise are shades of gray splashed with silver. The long narrow strip of green breathes sweet-scented sighs and clusters of dates hang unseen in the twilight exuding a divine, intoxicating aroma. The branches are tipsy and sway softly in the roofs of the palm trees, where the primeval fragrances are blended and lovingly scattered to the four winds.

My legs are in the cool refreshing water. People of the River, they have hurled the dam into your vast body and bruised it. They have raised it up over your solemn timeless melody. Be strong, mighty meandering river, for I am like you. The dam has destroyed my life. I was born the year it was built, and what an evil omen that was. The dam drove Siyam from the village. It has filled me with deep sorrow and made me suffer great loss. People of the River, smash the dam to pieces. Flex your muscles in anger. Bring forth an invincible flood, not around the sides but headlong into the high wall. Smash it down into a thousand and one bricks. Carry away the remnants of its destruction and scatter them far and wide. And the last brick, down there, let it crash into their salty sea where the mansion is that keeps Siyam the servant in his pressed gallabiya and his red cummerbund. Let the last brick land on the pale-faced Greek girl.

The mail boat anchored at the jetty and the gang-plank was lowered. The migrants came down carrying parcels of food and clothes. Their families were waiting with their camels and donkeys. Mothers hugged their sons, and wives were too shy to announce their desire and deprivation in public. I knew Siyam was not among them. I knew, but I was still there with everybody to watch. Mahjoub was wearing a gentleman's suit. He walked down the gang-plank with a great show of concern that the water might wet his clothes. He stole furtive glances at me and smiled conceitedly. I smiled back but inside I was mocking him. Full of pretension, he walked delicately so the sand wouldn't spoil his shoes. I thought to myself, "Mister Mahjoub, you are a ridiculous sight. You've abandoned our gallabiya and got yourself all dressed up in a northern suit. You've thrown away the skullcap and the noble turban and put on a red fez the color of a monkey's backside. Just look at the way you're walking on the sand. You're neither a southerner nor a northerner, neither one of us nor one of them. You're pouring with sweat and hopping like a crow. You've neither the grace of a sparrow nor the spirit of a wagtail."

Before sunset I went down to the river with a new generation of young women to fill the water jugs. Skinny Kalthouma was by my side. Klow To rode up on his stick donkey. In one hand he held the reins, in the other a piece of cucumber at which he nibbled. "You're a young man now, Klow To," I said, "but you're still stupid." He thrust himself into our midst and the girls started to laugh. They lowered the jugs into the water and Klow To turned to me. We faced one another and laughed. He moved toward me with his squint eyes. My heart fluttered, good news at last. We all leaned over. Klow To was staring at me. He said, "Congratulations to your groom," and handed the piece of cucumber to Kalthouma. Her face filled with joy. My heart sank into a pit of despair. The girls pinched Kalthouma. They were delighted, and envious. Kalthouma leaned farther forward as if to make her emaciated breasts more full, and Klow To took his treat. Klow To was still looking at me. I yelled at him, "You're lusting after me, you squint-eyed bastard, but you won't give me the good news." He took his dues from Kalthouma then ran up the bank and mounted his stick donkey. Behind him the end of the stick furrowed the sand.

Next winter the wedding of Fatim Nafisa, daughter of Simple Saleh, will be held. Nafisa said to me, "You'll dance at Fatim's wedding like you've never danced before, Asha. She's my daughter, your friend's daughter."

Aaah, another generation getting married. How long shall I be the one whose dance lights up other people's weddings? One generation after another, they hang the disk of the Almighty on their foreheads, married while I still wait. Shall I dance at the wedding of Fatim, the daughter of a man who was passionately in love with me? How long must I play the singed moth just to make the village happy? The women say that time has not chased Asha Ashry's beauty away. They do not know that I am struggling not to wither in front of their very eyes. A great dryness has taken hold of my heart and my liver is parched. For years, I have hidden the torment in my bowels lest the color of starvation show in my face and drive out its beauty, lest it be consumed by the ravages of time like the dam consumed our land, and that I might wear the disk of the Almighty . . . and marry Siyam.

Hundreds of times the mail boat came south, then went back down to the north. Siyam, the fool, did not come. Except for the letter every year to my father, he had completely abandoned me. He said he was coming, but he never did. He had drunk the salty water, even after Anna Korty warned him: "Siyam, beware of the salty water. It won't quench your thirst. It will make you more thirsty and sap your strength." Aaah . . . if only you had worn Anna Korty's advice like a ring in your ear, you would have come to rescue me and save yourself. The people in the village are talking. They've been blaming my father and my uncles. The women never stop gossiping, Siyam. The girls are grieving over me. Such beauty, they say, Asha Ashry's roseate milk, wholesome as fresh silt, sweet as candied dates, soft as butter, is drying up here while Siyam spends his time with seaside girls and the Greek nanny! You fool, you'll find no comfort there. You will return.

Klow To came running up on his stick donkey. He was waving a piece of paper. He stopped in front of me panting, his eyes on my breasts. My heart fluttered: good news. He gave me the paper. It was wet. He didn't utter a word. The joy carried me away. I laughed and I spun around and around and hugged the paper. At last . . . Siyam . . . Siyam. How happy I was. "He's coming back on the mail boat," I sang, "Oh, you beautiful mail boat, you will come back to the south with Siyam. The beak on your back will breathe forth a billowing green cloud, dancing like the perch. No black smoke after today." I bent over to give Klow To his treat, but he had disappeared. I pressed the piece of paper hard against my bare heaving chest, and a single icy tear slid down the furrow between my breasts.

The letter came with the mail boat. Siyam was arriving on the next boat. I swam to the River People and told them the news. The perch danced and cavorted. I ran through the village and told the people. All the villagers were delighted.

That night the men gathered. Alarm began to spread. Those who had just arrived said Siyam was sick. He would be coming back on a stretcher with Simple Saleh looking after him.

My grandmother consoled me in her fragile embrace, her fingers and feeble breath on my crumpled hair. "Patience, my granddaughter, patience. What is written must come to pass. You must endure your lot, Asha. Siyam's belly has filled with sea water and northern alcohol." I rested my head against her shoulder, and said softly "Anna Korty, you will cure him. You will draw the salty dampness from his back with cups of air and fire. With the bleeding-blade, you will cut his forehead and his calves, and the tainted blood will flow. You will rub his body with vinegar and red spirit, with castor oil and mountain herbs. You will wrap him in blankets till his cells spew up the scent of the Greek girl and spit out the corruption of the city."

A glorious morning. I couldn't find Klow To anywhere. I'd been looking for him a whole week. Then I saw him on the sands of the farky riding his stick donkey. I yelled, "Hey, Klow To, come here. The mail boat's late. When will it arrive? Say something. What? It's on the bottom of the river? I'll throw this stone at your head if you mean to bring me bad luck, you cross-eyed devil."

Fast camels relayed the news of the accident. Screams went up in village after village as the camels moved south with the news. The women tore their clothes in grief, and hearts bled. The camels arrived. The mail boat had sunk opposite the statue of Ramses at Abu Simbel.

Everyone from the village gathered in a black throng on the banks of the river. The women were wailing and a terrible anxiety was in the eyes of the turban wearers. A boat arrived, its sail bowed in mourning, carrying the survivors from our village. The women let out great screams. They

put the palm of one hand on their heads and beat on it with
the other and screamed, wayyy . . . wayyy . . . wayyy. Before
the village was sure who had survived and who had departed,
I knew. I leapt onto the boat. I grabbed Simple Saleh by the
scruff of the neck. We almost fell in the water. "Where's
Siyam? You were with him? Why did you let him drown?
You should have drowned and let Siyam return to me.
You're simple; he's tall and proud." They pulled me off him.
Scraps of his flesh were under my nails and between my
teeth. There was crying on the bank, and Saleh and the rest
of the survivors were crying on the boat. They swore that
the sinking happened in an instant, swift and violent like a
terrible nightmare. "Siyam did not help us to rescue him.
He didn't even try to get up from his stretcher. He sank to
the bottom as if resigned to his watery fate. We did not
find his body."

Each village lost one or more. Every hamlet, the whole of
the Nubian south, was one great funeral for the victims of
the disaster.

I will never marry you, Siyam. I will never lay my head on
your chest like our two trees, the palm tree lovers.

Night came. Crowds offering condolences. The women
and girls all around me weeping and screaming, barefoot,
pair after pair facing one another, their hands in the air
waving their black veils. They chanted the dirge to a sad
tune that tore your soul apart. The right foot moved one
step to the side and then returned before the left one
moved to its side. Then the pairs of facing women moved
forward and embraced one another, laying their heads on

their partners' shoulders in tearful lament. Then they drew apart screaming, raising their hands to brandish their veils at the dome of the sky, at the fate of the drowned. Hundreds of women praising the virtues of the deceased and the melodious anguish of the dance of the bereaved upset the peace of the universe, and it broke its silence to join in their suffering.

The sheikh of the mosque was furious. He reviled the women: "God's curses be upon you and Hellfire your reward. You scatter sand on your heads and lament the dead!" Not a single woman heeded him, for no man could feel how deep their grief was that night. The awesome sorrow in the hearts of the women was unbearable. The women, who were as stable and solid as a pillar of rock, had lost their stability. They wept for Siyam. They wept at the fate of their husbands and sons in exile. Terrified of an unknown future, they bemoaned their lot, the migration of the men to the north, to the painted white women of the north, and the danger of seduction. They were left with the burning heat of the sun and the parched earth of their drowned land, and their own inevitable destiny, one day to migrate in the wake of their menfolk toward the salty sea once the big dam has been completed and the rest of their land is swallowed up.

What has become of our villages where the Nile reigns? What has happened to our villages where the wolf roams in the mountains, the scorpion scurries over the sand, and the snake crawls? Our villages were once so safe.

The looks of sympathy and apprehension annoyed me. I slipped away and ran to the edge of the village. The sea of night had blackened the sands of the farky beneath me, and I swept down into it like a bird. I squatted down, shaking violently. The girls caught up with me. They approached through the darkness. I laughed and stood bolt upright like a phantom. I moved in quick short steps. The girls were astonished. "Asha Ashry has gone mad," they cried, "Who would dance the perch dance at the funeral of the one she loved? She's mad." They took me back to the village. I got away and ran to the palm tree lovers. I embraced the slender male tree. I embraced him until his barbed scales dug into my flesh. Their hands could not free me. They had to tear me away.

They wanted me to cry so that my bulging eyes would fall back into their sockets. The girls insisted on hugging me and weeping into my ear. I will not cry. Is Siyam crying? Siyam has drowned? How? How could Siyam, the river swimmer, drown, O women of the south? He must be teasing, tall and proud. He's teasing. He knows the village has had the life sucked from it. He went over to the River People where every pleasurable delight is seen and heard, where aragi flows in abundance, and no amount however great will give you a headache. I'll wait for him. I'll wait for him. He spends the night dancing with the water genies. I won't join in the funeral dance. I will not brandish my veil in the air or shake my fist at fate.

The weddings were delayed. The plumpness of my body wasted away, and in a few days my skin became wrinkled.

The tears were held back behind a dam of despair, and they welled up inside me and drowned my heart. They soaked my flesh and seeped through my bones to the marrow. The nights were black, the moon waning. I avoided our people and the River People. I howled like a wolf and ran off time after time to the drowned valley and the river. They always caught me and locked me up. I would shake and bellow and foam at the mouth. I would only be quiet with Anna Korty. She would stroke my hair and weep and say, "They've locked you up, Asha, just like they locked up your grandmother. Asha, be patient, be patient. Remember God's kindness. Patience, patience."

The pale weddings began. They seemed to have forgotten Siyam. The weddings had to be held before the men went back to the north. The first one was that of Fatim, daughter of Nafisa and Simple Saleh. No one waited for Asha Ashry to dance the perch dance, to get the men drunk without aragi, to make them high without bango. Everyone in the village was there. The relatives of the drowned remained on one side, in silence. It was a disfigured celebration. The mail boat disaster weighed heavy on their souls. The light from the lamps and torches was a ghostly yellow. Hands clapped weakly and the tambourines uttered dejected beats that fell limply to the ground and did not rock the virgins' cells or resound through the night to echo in the mountain tops. The wolf let out a mocking howl, the hyena scoffed sarcastically, and the viper slept soundly.

My mother was next to me in the yard of our house. Anna Korty was lying down, about to doze off. When night fell, they went to sleep. My two guards were oblivious; I lay on my back. He forgot for so long, and when he remembered, he died. The stars were inflamed eyes. The sky was wet with dew and its heavenly lanterns grew dim as my eyes filled with tears for the first time since Siyam drowned. I stifled the convulsions so as not to wake the sleepers, and I slipped away. I stopped by the last hanging house. I looked at the drowned valley below me, eaten up by the flood. "What have they done to you, our river? They made you devour our plantations! Ah, the eternal hamboul amid the shallow lake. I can still make it out. It is like molten gold flowing inexorably northward, with the stars reflecting upon its surface like silver turbans. They are the turbans of the River People."

A winter mist passed beneath the stars and shrouded the thigh of the western mountain, as it bent down to drink from the water. The turbans vanished. "O God . . . O Prophet . . . O Messenger." The lid was taken off the river, the translucent sheet removed. I gasped. My body was tense. One palm on the top of my head, the other beating down on it. I screamed: "Wayyy . . . wayyy . . . wayyy." The cover was drawn back. The River People were calling me, and Anna Asha, . . . and Siyam. I ran back to Anna Korty's house. The stone alleyways were empty, the houses all quiet. Everybody was at Nafisa's daughter's wedding. I went into my grandmother's house. I kissed the wall that separated it from Siyam's house. I embraced it, and my whole being shook uncontrollably. In Anna Korty's room was the inlaid chest. I opened it and pulled out from among the gold objects the disk of the Almighty. I fastened it so it hung on the middle of my forehead. The necklace came down to my waist. The gold covered me. Ah, a perfect bride I was. I laughed with joy. "Tonight I will be married to proud Siyam." I went over to the bed, kicked off my sandals, and climbed up to take the sword off the wall. I brandished it in the air and sang in a hoarse voice choked with salty tears, "Raise your sword, O groom. Raise up your sword for your guests. Raise up, O groom, your sword for your guests."

Anna Korty turned over and woke up. "Where is Asha?" She surveyed the yard with her tired eyes. Holding up her bent body on her stick, she went to look through the tiny cramped rooms. "Where is Asha?" She kicked her daughter. "Where's your daughter? Where's Asha? Something terrible's happening."

They hurried over to Nafisa's daughter's wedding. Maybe she couldn't resist the perch dance. "Where is Asha, girls?" they asked. "You men, have you seen Asha? You southern drunkards with your aragi. You, stoned higher than the dam. Where is Ashry? Sober up! Where is Asha Ashry?" She wasn't among the crowd. They rushed back to the house, her father in front with her uncles and her terrified mother trying to keep up with them. "She's not in the yard." They went into the rooms. No one. In Korty's room they found the inlaid chest open, with all the contents scattered around. An uncle cried: "The gold's gone." The mother said, "But where's Asha?" Anna Korty went toward the bed.

Asha's sandals were overturned. "The sword! She's taken the sword!" Anna Korty took the veil off her blood-red hair and waved it wildly at the ceiling. "Get moving if you call yourselves men!" she cried. "Quick. Down to the river past the two palm trees. All of you. Asha Ashry has gone to the River People."

The mother let out a great howl.

They all headed for the lake of sadness. A stream of people flowing down the mountainside. Everyone understood. Asha Ashry had gone off to drown. The father, the uncles, and the men led the way while the women brought up the rear. The mother was shrieking. Her screams, like black lightning, rent the heavens. Behind them all the grandmother came, urging her bent body forward. She would have fallen flat on her face were it not for her stick.

Asha Ashry neared the deep hamboul. The water reached the tops of her thighs. She dragged her legs through the flood water and the smothered fertility of the thick silt.

Her hand was raised, waving the sword, and she sang mournfully, "Raise up, O groom, raise up, O Siyam . . ." She stumbled, then righted herself, laughing and weeping and continuing her song, ". . . your sword for your guests." The reflection of the stars on the water sparkled in her eyes. "To the Prophet we give praise." Her sighs were choked with tears. "To al-Mustafa we give praise. We give praise and ask for protection." The Great Star was the disk of the Almighty on the brow of the water. "The River People will sing our wedding song. To the Prophet we give praise, to al-Mustafa we give praise. The perch himself will dance for us, Siyam." Asha pressed on. "We give praise and ask for protection." Her chest pounded from exhaustion. She heard voices behind her in the distance calling, "Asha . . . Asha . . . Ashry, where are you? . . . Asha, where are you? . . . Asha!" Hoarse cries in the throats of the men. Sharp cries in the throats of the women. Their cries, set loose like deranged arrows, pierced the silence of the night, and ruffled the surface of the water. Heart-rending cries in the darkness as Anna Korty dragged her tired body onward.

Asha could make out her grandmother's voice. She stopped and looked around. The lamps and flaming torches and the flowing white gallabiyas descended from the heart of the mountain to the drowned plain. Soon they would be at the palm tree lovers. Amid all their din, she was aware only of Anna Korty's tearful pleas: "Find her, for God's sake find her." But Asha moved on resolutely against the hamboul. The sword danced above her. The gold jingle-jangled as it jumped about against her body in time with the silver turbans dancing on the hoary surface of the water, which rose inexorably. The waves cast the reflection of the turbans into her eyes and flung their spray against her face to mingle with her tears.

The children stood in long rows on both sides of the palm lovers. The water was up to their legs. The villagers continued to drag their bodies through the flood water. The lamps and the torches were held up high. A few boats moved through the water, searching, each with a lamp hanging at its prow. The mixture of men and women dissolved in the maelstrom. Some plunged into the hamboul, searching in the thick oppressive darkness. The towering black mountains around them increased the torment of their grief. The lamps and torches were unable to cast more than hopeless tremors of light. The croaking frogs fell silent, the crickets' chirping ceased and the shrieks of the mother and the other women died away.

As soon as someone thought they saw a dark patch floating, all hands would point to it, and the screaming would start again. Then they would discover that it was only a mirage brought on by their despair. They led the mother away. She continued screaming from the depths of her heart.

Next to the rows of children, Anna Korty had abandoned her stick. She knelt down, and the water came up to her chest. Her crooked body fell forward till the stream of water touched her face. She lowered her hands and scooped up the black stagnant mud mixed with fertile silt. She raised it above her head, and the water trickled through her fingers onto her fiery hennaed hair. She smeared the silt on her head and wailed in a faint, slaughtered voice, "Asha Ashry has gone. Asha Ashry has gone to the River People."

Glossary

A = Arabic; N = Nubian

adamir (N): Human beings.

adila (N): Farewell; return safely.

amon dugur (N): The evil inhabitants of the river.

amon nutto (N): The good inhabitants of the river.

Amsheer (A): The sixth month of the year, from early February to early March.

angareeb (N): A bed made of palm stalks.

aragi (N): A clear alcoholic spirit distilled from dates.

ashry (N): Beautiful.

bango (A): Marijuana.

Baramhaat (A): The seventh month of the year, from early March to early April.

Barmouda (A): The eighth month of the year, from early April to early May.

bey (A): An Egyptian aristocrat.

bismillah (A): In God's name.

damo (N): There is no ———.

dulka (N): A kind of fragrant oil.

farky (N): A depression in the land along the edge of the river, which is filled with water during flood time.

Fatiha (A): The opening chapter of the Qur'an.

gallabiya (A): A long loose flowing garment worn, in different styles, by men and women.

garri (N): Foolish, ridiculous.

gorbati/-ya (N): A pejorative term for anything non-Nubian.

hamboul (N): The river course.

ibibibib (N): An exclamation of surprise.

ibiyuuuu ibiyu (N): An exclamation in response to tragedy, particularly death.

ibn (A): Son.

immmmm (N): An exclamation of derision or contempt.

ittir (N): A soup made from the green leaf of the Jew's mallow; *mulukhiya* in Arabic.

ka kummo (N): This phrase negates what precedes it.

kabid (N): A kind of bread.

kaseer (N): Tall, multi-layered, white turban.

Kiyahk (A): The fourth month of the year, from early December to early January.

kum ban kash (N): An onomatopoeic expression to suggest a wedding.

mas kag ru (N): Greetings.

omda (A): The village headman; mayor.

shadoof (A): An irrigation device used to raise water from the river.

shaw-shaw (N): Gold head bands hung with beads.

Touba (A): The fifth month of the year, from early January to early February.

uburty (N): Ashes, soot.

wo nor (N): Exclamation of praise to, or fear of, God.
al-Salaam (A): One of the ninety-nine names of God.
ya salaam (A): An exclamation of great approval.

Modern Arabic Literature
from the American University in Cairo Press

Ibrahim Abdel Meguid *Birds of Amber* • *Distant Train*
No One Sleeps in Alexandria • *The Other Place*
Yahya Taher Abdullah *The Collar and the Bracelet* • *The Mountain of Green Tea*
Leila Abouzeid *The Last Chapter*
Hamdi Abu Golayyel *Thieves in Retirement*
Yusuf Abu Rayya *Wedding Night*
Ahmed Alaidy *Being Abbas el Abd*
Idris Ali *Dongola* • *Poor*
Radwa Ashour *Granada*
Ibrahim Aslan *The Heron* • *Nile Sparrows*
Alaa Al Aswany *Chicago* • *The Yacoubian Building*
Fadhil al-Azzawi *Cell Block Five* • *The Last of the Angels*
Liana Badr *The Eye of the Mirror*
Hala El Badry *A Certain Woman* • *Muntaha*
Salwa Bakr *The Golden Chariot* • *The Man from Bashmour* • *The Wiles of Men*
Halim Barakat *The Crane*
Hoda Barakat *Disciples of Passion* • *The Tiller of Waters*
Mourid Barghouti *I Saw Ramallah*
Mohamed El-Bisatie *Clamor of the Lake* • *Houses Behind the Trees* • *Hunger*
A Last Glass of Tea • *Over the Bridge*
Mansoura Ez Eldin *Maryam's Maze*
Ibrahim Farghali *The Smiles of the Saints*
Hamdy el-Gazzar *Black Magic*
Tawfiq al-Hakim *The Essential Tawfiq al-Hakim*
Abdelilah Hamdouchi *The Final Bet*
Fathy Ghanem *The Man Who Lost His Shadow*
Randa Ghazy *Dreaming of Palestine*
Gamal al-Ghitani *Pyramid Texts* • *The Zafarani Files* • *Zayni Barakat*
Yahya Hakki *The Lamp of Umm Hashim*
Bensalem Himmich *The Polymath* • *The Theocrat*
Taha Hussein *The Days* • *A Man of Letters* • *The Sufferers*
Sonallah Ibrahim *Cairo: From Edge to Edge* • *The Committee* • *Zaat*
Yusuf Idris *City of Love and Ashes*
Denys Johnson-Davies *The AUC Press Book of Modern Arabic Literature*
In a Fertile Desert: Modern Writing from the United Arab Emirates
Under the Naked Sky: Short Stories from the Arab World
Said al-Kafrawi *The Hill of Gypsies*

Sahar Khalifeh *The End of Spring*
The Image, the Icon, and the Covenant • *The Inheritance*
Edwar al-Kharrat *Rama and the Dragon* • *Stones of Bobello*
Betool Khedairi *Absent*
Mohammed Khudayyir *Basrayatha*
Ibrahim al-Koni *Anubis* • *Gold Dust* • *The Seven Veils of Seth*
Naguib Mahfouz *Adrift on the Nile* • *Akhenaten: Dweller in Truth*
Arabian Nights and Days • *Autumn Quail* • *The Beggar*
The Beginning and the End • *Cairo Modern*
The Cairo Trilogy: Palace Walk, Palace of Desire, Sugar Street
Children of the Alley • *The Day the Leader Was Killed*
The Dreams • *Dreams of Departure* • *Echoes of an Autobiography*
The Harafish • *The Journey of Ibn Fattouma* • *Karnak Café*
Khan al-Khalili • *Khufu's Wisdom* • *Life's Wisdom* • *Midaq Alley* • *Miramar*
Mirrors • *Morning and Evening Talk* • *Naguib Mahfouz at Sidi Gaber*
Respected Sir • *Rhadopis of Nubia* • *The Search*
The Seventh Heaven • *Thebes at War* • *The Thief and the Dogs*
The Time and the Place • *Voices from the Other World* • *Wedding Song*
Mohamed Makhzangi *Memories of a Meltdown*
Alia Mamdouh *The Loved Ones* • *Naphtalene*
Selim Matar *The Woman of the Flask*
Ibrahim al-Mazini *Ten Again*
Yousef Al-Mohaimeed *Wolves of the Crescent Moon*
Ahlam Mosteghanemi *Chaos of the Senses* • *Memory in the Flesh*
Mohamed Mustagab *Tales from Dayrut*
Buthaina Al Nasiri *Final Night*
Ibrahim Nasrallah *Inside the Night*
Haggag Hassan Oddoul *Nights of Musk*
Muhammad al-Mansi Qandil *Moon over Samarqand*
Abd al-Hakim Qasim *Rites of Assent*
Somaya Ramadan *Leaves of Narcissus*
Lenin El-Ramly *In Plain Arabic*
Ghada Samman *The Night of the First Billion*
Rafik Schami *Damascus Nights*
Khairy Shalaby *The Lodging House*
Miral al-Tahawy *Blue Aubergine* • *Gazelle Tracks* • *The Tent*
Bahaa Taher *As Doha Said* • *Love in Exile*
Fuad al-Takarli *The Long Way Back*
M.M. Tawfiq *A Naughty Boy Called Antar*
Mahmoud Al-Wardani *Heads Ripe for Plucking*
Latifa al-Zayyat *The Open Door*